SHAMEFUL ACTS

HAMLIN GAGE

BLUE MOON BOOKS
NEW YORK

Shameful Acts
© 2000 by Blue Moon Books, Inc.

Published by
Blue Moon Books
An Imprint of Avalon Publishing Group Incorporated
245 West 17th Street, 11th floor
New York, NY 10011-5300

Second Blue Moon Books edition 2004

ISBN 1-56201-419-6

9 8 7 6 5 4 3 2 1

Printed in the United States of America
Distributed by Publishers Group West

Introduction

Academically, a psychologist would approach a book like "Shameful Acts" with several misgivings, and we were no exception. The fluttering pendulum of existentialism has released two previously celled spectres, both of which could become ogres if improperly nurtured. One being the immensely intriguing science of morbid psychology, the other being recent Supreme Court decisions as to the license granted to creative writers and general phases of the communications medium, entotal.

Four letter words do not make lewd literature, nor can honestly presented vagaries of mind and body be villified as obscene. In this book, Hamlin Gage, whom

I know to be a most scholarly and unobtrusive gentleman, has taken a period of English history, specifically populated by sundry elements of a blossoming age. It was the age of massive class distinction, open toilets for both sexes, poverty, riches and the Hellfire Club. The heroine, if one can be found, is a talented girl, the idol of the London theater, supposedly sophisticated but actually suffering from the peculiar morality of the Victorian era, which created monstrous barriers to reality while it privately dealt in the most gruesome intimacies of human relationships. In this atmosphere of unrestrained licentiousness, her own libido broke the leash of nonentity and assumed its true schizophrenic form. Marlene de la Sage was a schizoid of the most avid nature.

It is also a psychological truth that were it possible for an accomplished therapist to anticipate the origins of a schizoid, he might direct both halves of the delinquent personality into positive chanels. With Marlene, her split character evolved among people and situations which by their very nature, could only lead to disaster. Being an actress of sensitivity and talent, she was only able to react in extremes, to the eventual surrender of her senses to the physio-psychic influences of her associates.

We have often debated the degree of sadism required to turn an average mentality into a depraved beast. Again the psychological truth that if sadism is an instinct, it flourishes best where opportunity and reception permit a monumental growth of the physical expression. Under other circumstances, Jan Macklin, the brutal whipmaster, might have simply been a mean father or a nasty husband. As over-seer of a near-serfdom, employed by a loose-living member of the Victorian gentry, he was permitted to advance his sadistic inclinations at will. His fondness for a whip was fetishism; being a man of great power and of an impressive physical stature, he needed no weapon nor device with which to inflict agony on his subjects.

We feel Hamlin Gage departed honesty when he assigned Tillie Fedren the role of a bisexual. It seems to be a device by which he exposed Marlene de la Sage to the extremes of sensualism, to no real point. She had already succumbed to a type of phallic worship, not uncommon among mature females, and she had permitted her daughter to be ravished without undue protestations. She is pictured as a most unsophisticated mentality, with small chance for exterior inspiration in the more finessed degree of sexual experience. She is interesting, psychologically, only in her total commitment to licentiousness. In making such a statement, one lays oneself open to general attack; the daily newspapers are resplendent with accounts of unsophisticated women who are revealed as grotesque exponents of every sexual extreme on the very long list.

This book is so cleverly written that one feels at various times an empathy for even the most violently animated characters. The reader should feel no guilt for such empathy, because in one form or another, we are all pathetically involved with anti-social instincts and pathological desires. If one needs to choose one character in this novel to nourish in sympathy, choose Mary Fedren, the despoiled twelve-year-old girl who could in those years face only one future. Rural England, at the turn of the century, would have hanged her in pious glee for her vengence upon Frederick Tensington II.

3

Shameful Acts

We do not think "Shameful Acts" is a pleasant tale because it compounds degeneracy and lays bare the beast that lies dormant in every human being, with diligent disregard for the average people among whom the perverted mentalities cavorted. This is legitimate in that many novels deal only with average people, disregarding the warped mentalities which abound in every level of society.

A few years ago, this sensitive writing could have succeeded in being only a bore because without the impact of unrestrained verbiage and total frankness, the psychological exposures would have seemed inadequately justified and the unemotional behavior patterns would have appeared to be contrived. For untold centuries, people have "fucked"; it was not until the dubiously exalted era of Christianity coupled cohabitation to "love" that mankind began to frown upon the free expression of its inherent desires. Tillie Fedren's plaintive philosophy of sensualism is profoundly true; in each libido there is a segment of sensualism totally separated from the socio-sexual theme by which most people are required to live. She thought it only applied to women because she was a primitive female, only slightly affected by her other inadequacies. Hamlin Gage never once revealed what any of the principals thought about the standards of morality as applied to other people.

This is a sound formula for truth. Our politics, religions and academic achievements leave no room for exterior estimation of psychic evaluations. Modern society insists that for survival, we must talk out of both sides of our mouth. Hamlin Gage is dealing with primitive emotions, primitive lusts and fundamental desires. His people seek, speak, and act in private interests. The raw edge of reality, no matter how brutal, is truth and only receives its horrific labels in the mouths of hypocrites.

"Shameful Acts" is not a therapeutic novel. It will cure no one of vagaries, nor will it stand as a monumental guide to querulous mentalities. It is, however, a remarkable example of understanding and those who are frightened by its frankness and bare exposures, may well be secretly suffering from the very elements it dares to reveal.

It is not a book for children nor the tremulous. As a novel, it avoids the burden of authenticity. It plays with coincidence and avoids tedious "arrangements" to justify time, place and circumstance. It must be of prime importance to anyone objectively interested in morbid and practical psychology.

Albert G. Lowen, Ph.D.

one

He stopped only a moment at the door of the cottage and without knocking, swung the plank barrier open to peer into the dusky, one-room house. No one was there and Jan Macklin had expected no one. He knew Joseph Fedren was a half kilometer distant, crabbing the barley field, and this was Thursday, Tillie's washday. Jan turned down the path to the creek. He cast a giant shadow in the morning sun because he was a huge man. He strode leisurely although his mind speeded ahead of his boots. He shifted the whip coiled around his left shoulder and rubbed his bristled chin with a ham-like hand.

6

Thursdays he liked very much. A grouse rustled in the brush and he half raised the single shot birdgun in his right fist, then he went on. There would be better game by the creek. Not only was Tillie Fedren the best fuck on the Tensington Estate; her daughter, Mary, was a juicy morsel of beginning appreciation.

Tillie saw him first from where she knelt, rub-a-dubbing the sudsy sheets on the flat stone worn to a hollow by many years of Fedrens; three generations had lived and toiled and fornicated under the brow of the moor. Jo Fedren's grandfather had helped lay the first stone of the Tensington Manse. Now she straightened up, a square-shouldered woman in a homespun dress, sleeves rolled, bodice loose and her dark auburn hair flowing around her pretty face. She wiped her hands on the coarse skirt and swept back her hair. The gesture caused her big bold tits to push hard at the half-open front of her dress. Then Mary saw him. She was standing downstream a bit, knees deep in the cool creek, her own bare arms swishing a washed square of linen free of the strong lye soap. She was twelve, and very blond, slimly built but promising at hip and breast. A look of pain came over her freckled face. Jan ignored her.

He walked up to Tillie, his broad bulk overshadowing her. "Morning, Tillie," he said in his broad Scottish voice, then he put his left hand in the front of her dress and rolled her big tits with ungentle fingers. She didn't shrug away, she dared not. The plaited whip was over two meters long and the short triple lash was knotted. "Morning, Mary," he said to the girl in the stream. She nodded only.

Jan set the shotgun against a willow fork, then capped it with his broad-brimmed felt. The whip he changed from hand to hand as he removed his leather hunting jacket. He turned a rather handsome figure of some fifteen stone, his reddish hair cut long and slightly curled over his close set ears. He stood in a vain arch while Tillie stared at the significant bulge up the front of his corduroy breeches.

He sat down on a patch of sward and the whip suddenly came alive. Its length snaked out and wrapped twice around her bare left ankle and he pulled her to him, jerking her the last step so she tumbled into his grasp. She caught herself on him and he lowered her to the grass, his whip still wrapped around her leg.

"Be a bit gentle, Jan," she pleaded, and because he liked her tits free to his mouth and fingers, she unbuttoned it farther to save rent cloth and snapped off buttons. Chuckling, he spread the cloth and let her tits roll free, bulbous white globes tipped with large pink nipples, showing tiny nodules. He squared to her and she put her fingers to his fly and unbuttoned the strained cloth. Jan grinned; she couldn't possibly free his cock unless she unbelted him, but for a moment, she gripped the shaft to test the hardness and thickness with which she was totally familiar. The worried sulk left her face. Then she unbuckled his belt and opened his waistband and a small moan escaped her lips as his huge prick angled up in bobbing strength.

Tillie's fingers worked the thick foreskin back and allowed the broad scarlet head to distend in lusting. She frigged him slowly, her fingers firm, her motions practiced. Presently, she shuddered and scooped his massive sack of balls free of the loosened trousers. They seemed to float in sperm, and the hairy sack was heavy in her palm. Tillie raised to one elbow and intensified her caresses. The blue veins wandering around the wrist-thick shank pulsated as his prick distended to full erection. Still she played, fascinated by the monster organ and its vivid coloring. Jan idly fondled her tits and soaked in the sensualism. Suddenly, Tillie sat up and with agile haste, stripped out of her dress and hurled herself upon Jan, mumbling words of haste and excitement as he mauled her broad, full ass and solid thighs which she parted fully when he laid her naked body back on the grass. Now Jan put his hand to the broad thick patch of dark hair growing from her navel down and to each side to cover her inner thighs and from a bushy, up-humped blanket around her livid cunt. The plump lips were slightly parted, revealing her well developed clitoris and below that, the lobed protuberances of her inner labia. He ruffled the clitoris and chuckled at her gasp.

"You were waiting for me, weren't you?" he teased her, not referring to the day or to the time of the morning.

"You're a foul man but a lovely fuck," she said, smiling now as his fingers dug and penetrated her vagina with small care for the delicacy of the secret organ. "What is the girl doing?"

Jan raised his eyes to the girl standing in the creek. "I think she's pissing," he laughed. "And I see a hint of fuck-push in the weaving of her hips! She's your daughter, all right!"

Tillie laughed in beginning hysteria and turned slightly to hump to his fingers, and to reach his cock again. Jan's chest rose and fell with rising excitement. As he turned to her, she raised her upper leg and threw it over his hip, now tan and hard where his breeches had

9

lost ground. She made the coupling but not until she had satisfied some sexual stimulus by rubbing his pulsating prick over and around her quim, wetting the blood-filled head with her oozing vaginal fluids. He squirmed and she shifted and then he felt the snug kiss of the lobed labida. He urged and she urged and the lengthy cock between them gradually shortened as it worked its ecstatic way into her burning cunt. Snugged, she giggled and clung to him and they began to fuck with perfectly timed undulations, closing together to smooth her burning cunt. Snugged, she giggled and clung, pressing. Jan let his hands wander her body, one cupping her taut buttock, to press and knead and squeeze until she jerked. Then his fingertips found the rather profuse hairs that grew up the crack of her ass and he let his middle finger rub her anus. Again Tillie giggled and redoubled her hunching, trying to fit closer to his hairy groin and absorb the last centimeter of his organ.

They began to roll then, she back first, to gasp and grunt as his mounting body beat down at her pliable flesh, then Jan rolled over and she rode up, also gasping as her spraddled crotch settled hard on the hunching rod. Then Tillie was on her back again, legs high on either side of his waist as his powerful rump pumped up and down in deeper, slowing strokes. Her eyes closed, her red mouth gaped, and he could feel her inner straining, tensing as the driving cock concentrated her delight. As his body whipped, Jan rested inside in consciousness, holding his virility at a level that would extend the excruciatingly pleasant stroking as long as he desired to do it. His vanity swelled. He was a master cockman and could fuck her to death if he chose. Of the twenty wives and twice that many daughters who lived and toiled on the Tensington Estate, few had stayed with him and none as well as did Tillie. Only today, he had the other inspiration so he ground his belly to hers and felt her come up in orgasm, mewling in his mouth as he split her lips with his tongue and tasted her throat.

"Ah-eough, ah God, oh!" she husked, twisting and writhing as the frenzy pounded under him. He stared down at her ecstatic agony and deliberately jolted her when she seemed to coast. Then his rooting merely shook her relaxed body. Tillie lay with eyes closed, her face a pretty thing of placid surrender. One arm raised to cross her forehead and the other lay out in listless resting.

"You didn't——" she murmured.

"But I will, have no fear!" he said and reared to his knees, arms hanging. His cunt-wet prick gleamed brightly in the sunlight, up-angled from the wet mat of rust-red hair that coated his groin. The smell of Tillie came up to his nose and he sucked in a deep breath to ease his lungs. Then he looked out at Mary.

Her childish distress was obvious. She stood, feet well apart in the water, her body slightly bent at the hips. When her wide eyes perceived his attention, the hand curled tightly under her belly flew aside. Her mouth closed firmly, giving her face a look of shame. "Come here, wench," Jan ordered in a deep if gravelly voice.

"No! No, Jan!" Tillie cried, snapping up, her hand going to his prick. "No, not the little one! Me, Jan, me! Anything you want to do to me—no matter how many times, but not Mary! I beg you!"

Still grinning, Jan slammed the back of his right

hand across her face, spinning her half over into a wailing heap. He got to his feet, hitching at his falling breeches but not high enough to cover his strong bare ass and the gigantic out-thrust of his rigid cock.

"Come here, Mary," he commanded.

"No, Jan, no!" Tillie cried. "No! Take the whip to me—you like that! Beat me, kick me, fuck me as you like. Oh, God, no!"

In the creek, Mary turned as if to run. The whip swished out and wrapped around one of her arms. Jan jerked and pulled her stumbling and weeping to the creek bank. His left hand closed around her slim throat, not to choke but to hold her, motionless and afraid. He flicked the whip free of her arm and sent the last whistling to pop Tillie's left tit as she tried to rise to Mary's rescue. She screamed in agony and fell back, squirming, ripping her quickly scarlet breast with frantic fingers. She lay on one hip, weeping into her folded arm as Jan went to his knees and pulled Mary down into a writhing huddle against him. He fucked at her, jabbing her belly and chest with his pole-stiff cock while he tore at her dress and bloomers. She struggled, but to no avail. When he had her bloomers down, nearly securing her kicking legs, he turned her and sent his prick from behind up into her crotch.

"Mama, mama!" she screamed. "Mama, help me, help me!"

"Jan, no, no!" Tillie cried, but she did not rise.

He found the little cunt, a soft, inadequate slit in the squirming underbody. The pain of his jab made her legs move out, and he held her firmly and worked his ruthless cock in the softness, enjoying the smooth skin and diminutive contours, and finally, the feel of his prick nudged hard into the tiny vagina. Mary suddenly stilled, her breath a hot fast rushing from her slack mouth. His hand curled around and down and found his cock, wedged only a centimeter or two in the distorted slit, now turned into a painful circle. He hunched back and his fingers dug into the virgin cunt, to stretch and rip the tender flesh. Mary howled and wept and tried to wriggle away but he held her and finger fucked the blood-moist slot until it seemed more tractable. Then he put his prick to the wounded hole and with no hesitation, urged the head well in and up. Again, Mary seemed atrophied with pain. He clamped her to his torso and began to fuck, each stroke gaining more exquisite depth until almost half of his hand-length cock was coursing in the expanded sleeve. Impaled, Mary instinctively tried to ease her agony, and her legs spraddled out, to brace in the grass so she could twist and soften his brutal undulations. Blind with excitement, Jan fucked, but with reserve. He could have had cum the instant his prick entered the small cunt, but his mind toyed with his vanity. The girl was fucked, her first pains were over; he remembered how she had often stood and watched him hump her mother, cunt and bum, and he recalled her only minutes ago, standing in the creek with her fingers pressing her bloomers into the sensitive slit he had thoroughly turned into a cunt. He eased his lunging, shortly stroking the hot aperture, waiting to sense the moment when her budding female parts reacted as they must do. His first signal was her hand, coming to grip his forearm as it clamped her to his belly. Then her head lifted and the sobs became jerky, incomplete. After that, he felt her hips begin to move, the subtle helping twist. Her obvious response nearly shattered Jan's mind; for the first time in his adult memory, he had created a woman, and the mysterious blossoming from frightened child to squirming panting acceptance of his lust gave Jan Macklin a lordly, omnipotent feeling. Now she was mewling and grunting, and he hurt a little by deepening his dog-huching. But not for long did she gasp in pain. He felt under to learn how his cock was in the hot wet aperture, and he sent a finding fingertip under her ass to test the tiny wink of her asshole. Exactly like any other female bum he had tested. Mary's ass hole contracted and relaxed to his prick's coursing. She seemed not to feel his finger so he pressed inward, causing her a sudden jerk of awareness. Proof that Tillie had ceased her wailing and was watching came when his digging middle finger entered Mary's bum and Tillie gasped, "Oh, my God in Heaven!" Then he felt her hands, cool but nervous, feeling under his ass to the swinging tensing sack of balls, then on until Tillie's searching fingers moved up his prick to where her daughter's cunt lips dragged and sucked in with his sliding foreskin. He felt her tits hot against his shoulder and her breath burned his neck. He freed one arm and struck Tillie away, his animalistic instincts dedicated to the rape that was no longer a rape. Mary was like a small nymph in his grasp, rolling and humping of her own volition and Jan abruptly became aware of small rocks under his knees. He weighed forward on her and her legs folded, and he held as they fell to maintain the delicious imbedment of his cock. His body covered hers. except the out lick of her bare feet and the spread of her elbows. Her small ass, hung on his cock, reared up, rolling and bobbing. He supported some of his bulk on his forearms, now wrapped under her low belly and his fucking intensified with the new freedom. He mashed her nates under his belly and ground her thighs to the half-dirt, half-grass. He had no will to cum but he knew he could at any moment. His lust was mighty, but he held to his rhythm, waiting for the second signal that Mary had become a woman. He had no knowledge that she could or could not cum; he thought she was going to because her moaning tightened and became louder. Now her ass came up like a resilient ball when he made his limited withdrawals and she resisted his lunge until the size and weight of his prick became resistless. Waiting for the signal, he missed its warning and then he felt her jerk, downward then up and her belly against his arms had furious convulsions. Ruthlessly, he fucked on, and even when she lay under him in writhing lassitude, he held his jim to test her second responses.

"No Jan, she is done, done!" Tillie cried. "Give her a chance! Cum and be done with her!"

He laughed to frustrate Tillie but a moment later, he was trapped by his own delight in the milking sleeve. He felt it at the tip of his spine, then his balls tightened and the blue ecstacy began. The first spurt of jism was like tiny stones, coursing the expanding tube under his raging prick. He felt a dull pain at the head of his cock, now tightly snubbed to the limit of her little quim. Then he moved, releasing the dam and his jism shot and spewed and became a fire lining around his organ. He grunted and gasped, the relief after so long a fuck sapping his control for several seconds. His jism seemed endless in its flowing and the few short undulations he managed made gushing wet sounds in her vagina. She lay, panting and squirming and when he raised, his limping cock was sleek with cum and lightly pink with churned blood.

"You—you beast!" Tillie wailed. "My poor raped baby!"

He stared down at her bowed back and bended rump as she petted and comforted the trembling Mary. Jan thought of thrusting his prick into the hair-fringed asshole but he had left his jism and his strength in Mary. He wiped his cock on her discarded dress, then stood looking down at them both, his senses reeling with the lewdness he had so thoroughly enjoyed. Then he looked up at the sun and decided there was little time for more of the erotic delight. He urinated copiously, ears deaf to Tillie's belated weeping and Mary's little-girl words of shock and surprise. Slowly, he donned his jacket and hat, recoiled his whip and retrieved his shotgun.

"Tomorrow," he said. "I will put Joseph in the far field with the hoe."

Tillie turned and squared her shoulders. "You dare not! She is but a child!"

"She fucks like her mother, but with a tighter cunt," Jan laughed. "And she has your kind of cock hungry asshole, too! I will be at the cottage by ten. I am wont to try that one on the breadth of a bed!"

"No, Jan, no!" Tillie pleaded.

He placed his muddied field boot to the soft valley between her tits and shoved mightily. Tillie flew backwards, hooked her bare heel on a clump of creek mud and splashed, flailing and gasping into the cool water. Then Jan leaned down and patted the plump little buttocks. Mary turned her head to look up at him but he could not read her expression. He'd change it for her tomorrow, first by thrusting his cod into her mouth and then by a number of other gymnastics which pleased him to contemplate. He strode off the hill toward the Manse, most pleased with himself.

———————————

Mary rolled over to a flat-legged seat, her legs seemingly unwilling to close together. She watched the huge groundskeeper climb the slope; she hardly recognized the man whom she had learned to hate, not for his molestation of her but for the autocratic way in which he had always taken her mother. The word was fuck, and she had always thought a harsh, dirty word like fuck could have no other connotations, despite the fact that once it began, her mother seemed always to adore any brutality Jan Macklin could devise. Mary looked up at her mother, emerging from the creek, her white skin dripping with sparkling in the sun.

"Oh, mama!" Mary husked. "He has hurt me terrible!"

"Poor baby! Wade out and sit down in the water. It will cleanse you of his filth and ease your poor torn flesh." Tillie knelt to pass two gentle fingers down between her daughter's legs and into the blood-flecked slit, surprisingly closed, if quaking. Mary winced because there seemed to be a very sensitive place where her mother's touch was surprisingly welcome. Then she winced again as the fingers coursed slowly, searching along the raw and irritated inside of her place. "To the creek," Tillie finally breathed.

The water seemed bitterly cold, and Mary shivered as she held her skirt high and lowered her bottom into the stream. Instantly, she had to urinate which made a warm place in the water for a short moment before coasting downstream. Her part burned and tingled. She felt like vomiting and evacuating but the nausea soon left. Then her squat made her feel a different need, and she looked up toward the top of the hill. But the cruel, unfeeling man was over the rise. She swallowed, for a moment not sure of how she thought until she remembered his promise to be at the Fedren cottage at ten on the morrow. Her heart pumped strongly with sudden excitement.

He had left his shotgun in the broad hallway but the whip was still a promising coil over his left shoulder as Jan stood, hat in hand before Frederick Benning Tensington II. Jan had never decided whether he liked the heir to the Manse or not; he had liked his deceased father because Squire Tensington had not been of blue blood nor any of its annoying characteristics. Frederick was slim and possessed none of his father's ruggedness of body and mind, but he had quick eyes and made quicker decisions.

"All right, my man," Frederick said. "If the barley is in order, bring in several of your most dutiful men and make certain the gardens and terraces are in shape. An hour or so after tea tomorrow, my guests will start arriving from London. The housekeeper's man will require a wagon this afternoon so that provender may be obtained. Oh yes. Yourself be free of duties over the weekend. The nature of my guests in particular and I would have your whip and your scatter-gun on guard during the night. Do you understand?"

"Yes sir. I will do my best," Jan promised. He didn't mind the impersonal tone, even though he had known young Frederick for several years. And the trust placed in him by the suggested guard duty was pleasant; it would also give him a chance to peek at the antics of the gentry, and the gentry's ladies.

And with Joseph Fedren busily engaged with leaves and shrubbery clippings, his tryst at the Fedren cottage at ten in the morning would be undisturbed. With a respectful bow to his back, Jan went through the huge stone manse to the rear doors. He had little to do with the house which was amply supplied with servants but there was a favorite of his now acting as the pantry maid. He saw her at the entry to the service areas; he suspected that she had heard his voice in the echoing chambers.

"Ah, my winsome one," he said, chucking her under the chin. "Your tits look in fine fettle. Has that old rake, Gibson, been keeping them well pumped up? Not that the old fool has enough jism in his ballocks to pump up a kitten, but he'd try, I'm sure."

"I know not what jism is, so long have you avoided me, man!"

"Now, Belle! You know what important things I must do about the estate. But I thought often of your plump ass and greedy quim!"

"I'm sure! Everytime you thrust your cod into Wife Medwick you thought of me! Where go you now?"

"To my cottage," he replied, nodding through the wall in the direction of his house. "To rest before I take to the fields at one."

She shifted, her face flushing from hairline to the rise of her lush tits. "And who waits to help you rest?"

His thick eyebrows raised in indignation. "Why, Belle! To think that you'd accuse me of such perfidy!"

She looked back into the kitchens. "There is little here for me to do, at least until the master calls for lunch," she murmured.

He felt randy; the hour with Tillie and the girl had spoiled his need for adventure not at all. He handed the dark haired wench a big brass key. "Go first and quietly," he said.

She giggled, and with a flirt of her ample bottom, went out into the rear courtyard. Jan wandered into the kitchen and found a half of cold baked chicken in the cooling room. He took it and went slowly out, munching the great mouthfuls he took with evident relish. He was still licking his fingers when he approached the small cottage where he lived. The gate was open and when he got to the door, it too was ajar. Belle stood with her maid's cap off and her raven tresses hanging about her shoulders. She had also removed her peasant's blouse. He had almost forgotten how black her tit tips were, and he thought she had plumped some since she had quit the granary mill and moved to the kitchen of the manse. He closed the door and set the inside latch. She stood looking at him, her trembling a visible thing in the jelly-like bounce of her bold boobs.

He took off his hat and like a striking cat, slapped her across the tits with the rough felt. She gasped and spun, to fall backward on the hard-scrubbed planks of the cottage floor. Laughing heavily, he stooped and seized one of her ankles, lifting her nearly free of the floor. Her skirts fell back, the other leg kinked, and with brutal finger, he opened the neatly lipped cunt in the thick curly hair of her crotch. She giggled, and did some convulsive thing with her belly that set her quim to quaking. Jan dropped her and with deliberate fingers,

20

removed his wide leather belt. Methodically, then, he spanked her bare bottom, her back, and her tits, choosing whatever she turned to him in her writhing and twisting pleasure. She moaned and pleaded and panted and his cock came up until it lay snugly between his trousers and his belly. Presently, the belt began to really hurt her and she crawled to the broad feather bed against the wall. He followed her, with right and left blows to her bottom. She lay crying when he ceased his punishment to remove his boots and outer garments. Naked, huge and hairy, he bent and put his belt around her waist cinching it until she gasped for breath. He jerked her skirt off and tugged harder at the belt. Her small waist became tiny and her inner organs crowded up and down. She wailed and beat at her bulging tits. Jan notched the buckle tongue and spread her legs. The cruel belt had mostly crowded down. Her cunt was a bulge of scarlet flesh, ridged, dimpled and slightly gaping where the short inner lips hardened in anticipation. Her asshole was also pooched, the soft brown ring so distended the delicate inner pink showed bright. He raised her legs and hauled her to him as he half crouched at the edge of the bed, his cock distended in a waving stiffness. She yelped when he penetrated her cunt with the rigid pole, and he spread her upraised legs until the tendons stood out in strain from the white inner thighs. He fucked her deeply and slowly, laughing softly at the agony she showed each time his monstrous organ plunged into her disorganized body. Finally, Belle began to respond.

"I—I had almost forgotten!" she gasped. "You lovely fiend! Ah, Jan dear, your cock and your talent will ruin me yet!"

He hauled his prick free of the pulsating quim and turned her over, lifting her to hands and knees so her broad soft ass was bended and the nates properly parted. He placed his slippery prick to her asshole and worked it into minute snugging. Then he reached and with a jerk, released his constricting belt. Belle moaned as the belt relaxed and her belly dropped. Jan rammed his cock into her anus and as if swallowing, her bum absorbed his steaming prick to the hilt.

She screamed, softly and ecstatically and he reached under to seize her throbbing tits in his ungentle hands. He pulled and milked them as he bum-holed her and the girl bucked and writhed in frenzied joy. He paid no attention as to whether or not she had cum. She was a wild one, possessed of her own queer sensuality. He only wanted to fuck into a hard cum of his own; his knees were jittery and his back not fully recovered from the creekside orgy. His jism was strong, however and Belle wept with ecstasy as he lubricated her bowel with the sleek ejaculation.

Later, while she evacuated her bowel on his chamber pot, he let her wipe his cock clean and lick the final oozing drops of his curdled cum. He called her a fucking slut and a filthy bitch and she rubbed his prick in her thick hair and hummed a song of contentment against his groin. When he pissed, she guided the stream down between her tits and let it trickle over her belly and down over her hairy quim.

At five minutes to one, she dressed and left, giggling, pleading to him for a future tryst and panting with renewed passion. He lay down to what he thought was a well-earned nap.

two

This day there was no need for the usual bread and cheese, wrapped in a clean white cloth, because her daddy was going to work at the manse, and the kitchens there were always abundantly supplied with meat and bread and wine. Mary stood waving as her father walked up the hill, looking back occasionally to blow a kiss to her. She was trembling with excitement that was new to her childish mind. In three hours, he would come, unless his words were false or the master of the manse required his presence. Turning, Mary went back into the cottage where her mother was straightening the bed and picking up.

"Do you think he will really come, Mama?" Mary asked.

"Pray that he does not! And get about reading your lessons! I will hear your problems when I have done the breakfast dishes."

"Yes, Mama. And if he comes?"

"God in Heaven! One would think you wanted him to come!"

"I see you sneaking glances toward the hill each wash morning, Mama! What he does with you can not be so very awful or you would not laugh and wriggle as he does it, would you?"

Tillie sighed and sat down, staring at her daughter with puzzled eyes. Mary thought she had spoken a truth; together they had conspired to speak nothing of her adventure of the previous morning, and Mary delighted in this secret, just as she had clung tenaciously to her promise, made three years before, not to hint to her daddy the exciting acts committed on the banks of the wash-creek. Secrets were lovely to Mary. Her life was very staid, very uninteresting, except for washdays. Her nearest playmate lived nearly a kilometer distant and except for Sunday school, she mingled with the other children of the Tensington Estate very little. Three mornings a week she went to school, a terrifying place where she felt she was inferior. Proof that her mother believed the groundskeeper would come—and expected something extra—lay in the fact that this was a Friday and thusly a school morning. Mary was privately exuberant; the prospect of missing two frightening hours of reading, writing and figures was joyous and the secret longing to test the peculiar joys of yesterday again was making her head swirl with excitement.

"Mama, he is very big, isn't he?"

"Big?"

"His thing, I mean. Much larger than daddy's, I'm sure."

Tillie's eyes opened wide in surprise. Mary smiled. "But we all sleep here together, Mama! Of course I have seen it, more than once. It can not be as huge as Mister Macklin's because you do not moan and carry on when daddy's thing is in you, no matter where he puts it!"

Shocking her mother was fun. When Tillie sagged, her face in her hands, Mary didn't feel as devilish as she had thought. She went to her mother and put a slim arm over the bowed shoulders and pressed a kiss into the thick auburn hair. Impulsively, her mother's arm went around her, clinging. "My baby has become a—a woman, thanks to that hideous beast—and my own weaknesses! No. I will not let him—!"

"It's all right, Mama, it's all right!" Mary whispered. "I think I even liked—some of it!"

"Go—go read your lessons, my poor darling!"

It was difficult, but Mary managed to spend two hours staring at the thin, much used book, turning the pages as if she were reading, but really looking through the book and the table at the heroic figure of a big, red-complexioned man who stood half naked, his hairy groin and thighs a monstrous pedestal for the peculiarly intriguing column of white and scarlet flesh. She remembered every detail of its shape and size, from the thick hair growing at its root to the soldier-helmet head, spreading and pulsating with vivid hue. Her small fingers clasped and unclasped, forming a hollow which she imagined the big shaft would completely fill. There had been no time nor opportunity yesterday, but maybe today, in the seclusion of the cottage, he would let her feel of it and learn its secrets. As ten o'clock approached, Mary closed her book and sat shaking. Tillie was fussing a great deal; her mother's face was oddly strained, not soft as it usually was.

"Mama? It is nearly ten," Mary said, nodding toward the old brass clock above the stone fireplace.

Tillie nodded. She went to the cupboard and brought back a familiar pottery jar. Mary knew it contained goosegrease; it was used to ease bruises and cuts and sometimes, to water-tight her father's boots. Her mother put it on the table and removed the lid.

"Stand on your chair, Mary. Take down your bloomers."

"W-why, Mama?"

Tillie sighed. "Later, you will understand fully, I'm sure!"

Mary got to her feet on the chair seat, then she peeled down her cotton underdrawers and hung them neatly over the wicker chairback. Her mother then approached and raised her skirt, staring for a moment at her daughter's naked hips. Mary squirmed, it tingled some and felt very hot, but the swelling didn't hurt any more. Her mother took a generous two fingers of the slick, thick grease, then with one hand cupped around Mary's left buttock, introduced the greased fingers directly into Mary's slit. Mary gasped, then squirmed as Tillie worked the grease in and around, sometimes touching the good place, more often soothing the raw insides. Mary's knees kinked out in response to a touch; Tillie sent her two long fingers in very deep and coursed them in and out a number of times.

"Does it irritate you, Mary?"

"N-no. Some! Oh, Mama, whatever is the grease for?"

"To keep you from being torn and injured, Mary. Turn."

"T-turn?"

"Yes!" Tillie's hand insisted and Mary turned, her knuckles white as she clenched her hands around the skirt of her up-drawn dress. "Now, bend, very far. As if you were touching your toes!"

Mary bent forward, balancing as some strange headiness joined her confusion. She saw her mother's hand, the fingers scooped another blob of goosegrease. Then to Mary's shock, the cool grease was laid heavily to her bum hole. She tingled as her mother's fingers rubbed and pressed, each rub pressing deeper until suddenly, the finger went right in. "Oh, Mama!" Mary gasped as the strange sensation caused her belly to flutter. "Oh, Mama!" Then she was shivering with peculiar feelings running from her mother's two fingers in her bum to her middle chest. The fingers rotated and screwed themselves in and in until she could feel her mother's knuckles against the taut rounds of her bottom. The grease cooled the first burning and softened the ring of tight flesh. Mary swallowed hard as it ceased to be unpleasant. She wriggled, and Tillie did another half minute of the in-and-outing. Mary wanted to pee and when her mother finally slipped her fingers out of the soft, resilient hole, she wanted to evacuate.

"Mama! I have to—to go!"

"Yes, Mary. Go to the outside pot, then wash well and come back. There will be more to do when you are at ease."

Now, Mary understood. She sat naked across his bare thighs, her slim legs parted so his huge and delightfully warm cock thrust up to her quim, the head well buried in her greased canal. He was feeling her body, teasing the small pads with the tiny nipples, breathing hotly on her face. His belly was hard and heaving against her leg. The throbbing club in her quim felt very snug, but it did not hurt. Mary looked at her mother, standing with her back to the door, her naked body a trembling loveliness. Mary dared relax the tightness of her buttocks which action dropped her body so the starting cock pushed in until the thick foreskin formed a ring against the circle of her cunt. It felt very good and her fingers wriggled.

"Jack me off, little one," the groundskeeper said.

Mary looked at her mother. "What should I do, Mama?"

Tillie sobbed and came forward, going to her knees before Jan Macklin and her daughter. She put all five fingers to his prick and slowly began to frig the abundant skin. As she did this, Jan began to hunch slightly and Mary gasped at the sudden stretching in her belly Then the stretching enlivened some nice places. She giggled, causing her mother to moan softly.

"Is it good?" Jan demanded.

"It—it doesn't hurt," Mary conceded. "Is it meant to be good, sir?"

He laughed boisterously and hunched a bit harder. "See there, Till, old girl? You've taught your daughter badly! Yes, Mary, it is meant to be good. Let go, Till, and give her a chance to feel a man's cock getting up her! Do what your mother was doing, Mary."

Tillie moved back, her hand leaving the thick shank with obvious reluctance. Mary took hold, reaching down quickly. The prick was harder than she had thought and hot, and it throbbed delightfully. Again she giggled and shifted her bottom on his thigh. She wanted to raise her knees and when she started to do so, he cradled her back in his arm and several centimeters of his cock seemed to surge into her quim. "Ah, damme!" he gasped. "Come right into it like a bitch in heat! And I think she's getting it, Till! Look at her twist!"

Mary only half heard their low exchange of words, as if she were some prize animal at the Squire's Meet in Pennington. But it didn't matter. The same fierce feeling was coming on, as it had yesterday after the pain and fright had thinned. Her fingers speeded, her body twisted in excruciating eagerness. Abruptly, she couldn't stand it so she yelped and turned her face to his coarse shirt. The small thumping sent aches of pain and good coursing in her belly. She giggled as they slowed and humped down, gasping as the movement prolonged the thumpings.

"Pops her granny like a true country wench!" Jan laughed.

"Enough, enough!" Tillie panted. "Let her go, Jan! Have me! I need you, God help me, I need you now, now!"

His left hand came out and palmed her mouth with a loud smashing smack, knocking her to the floor, her legs akimbo, her tits jouncing. She dropped her chin to her breastbone and sobbed softly.

29

Mary wanted to cry for her mother, so cruelly treated, but the big club still moved in her quim. Then he lifted her and the abrupt emptiness was the most terrible feeling she could remember. His cock stuck up, wet and pulsing and when he stood, her body held to his thigh, it extended several centimeters past the thickness of her body. As she stared, Tillie lurched forward and took over half of the thick organ in her mouth and her lips worked furiously as if to finish the matter, once and for all. Jan laughed and hunched to Tillie's lewd greed. Mary trembled, frightened at the seeing fury between them, and her quim drooled to her inner thigh as she tensed in surprise.

Then Jan again struck Tillie, knocking her away. "No, you don't, Till! I'm going to teach her the whole schedule so don't you think you've fooled me a bit! Anyway, I'm thinking she likes all that's happened to her so far! Stay back, you jealous slut!"

Tillie cowered, her eyes not unlike those of a frightened hedgerow hare. A peculiar contest blossomed in Mary's mind; she loved her mother dearly, but somehow, she was pleased that the groundskeeper was so rough and domineering. She clung to him, quivering. He patted her small bottom and carried her to the big bed. Turned, at least so her mother could not see, Mary made bold to grip the huge prick laying against her side. The nakedness and the body heat was thrilling, and she suddenly wished her mother were elsewhere.

"Are we going to do it again?" she whispered.

His chuckle was reassuring, but his hand was suddenly on her bottom and his finger was pushing at her bum hole. His chuckle deepened. "The eyes weep but the mind was not blank!" he said. "Turn over, small one, and we will try your well-greased ass with a suitable instrument of testing!"

Eagerly, Mary spun in his grasp and pushed her little rump to his groin. His cock lay hard up against her bottom, and his belly was like a soft cushion. Then he moved her and she felt the cock, softly covered stiffness, nudge into her undercurves. She held her breath, identifying what she thought was going to happen with the queer ecstasy of her mother's application of goose-grease.

The agony sent scream after scream from her throat. The cock seemed like a tree, spreading her tortured anus, wedging her buttocks apart, but relentlessly driving in. She doubled, hurt that way and tried to stiffen, then the pain shocked her into total limpness. She heard his breath, mingled with growling glee, and she felt his huge hands holding her to him. The fire was deadly, the stuffing nearly impossible to bear. She sobbed and twisted but so deep and firm was the penetration that she could barely move. He was grunting now, each grunt accompanied by the impossible filling, each withdrawal only a moment of respite before the petrifying thrust. Mary lay, nerveless but feeling every wounding; somewhere her mother was weeping and cursing and behind her was the huge power of a gigantic man. She raised her upper leg, kicking to ease the concentrated pain. The fingers now at her quim were hard and insistent, sending pleasanter shocks to dull the bursting of her body. Then there was fresh agony as he jerked and hunched even harder. Mary yelped and groaned and tried to ease away but he held her and pumped the unstandable fire into her body until she lay gasping in a near faint. She had one childish, logical thought before the darkness claimed her; without the goosegrease, her bum hole would have been a shredded horror.

Jan stood, his shit and blood-smeared cock hanging out in a long, half-weary arc. He looked down at Tillie, clamped around his leg, her head down, her breath a rasp of either pain or passion. He wasn't fooled. He had fucked her cunt and bum for three years. He knew her nature, her insatiable love of a ruthless prick. She was a mother by nature and a slut by intent. He looked at the quiet little body, lying face down on the bed. Twelve or fourteen? He didn't know. "Are we going to do it again?" she had whispered. Her asshole was closed now, leaking watery brown. She had taken nearly the full length of his prick in her bum and of course, the full girth. It had been a fuck to Jan Macklin, only exquisite because his mind had raced lewdly ahead of his lust. With her heritage and tastes, ten years would bring her to her back under a plow horse. Another day, Monday perhaps because of Tensington's scheduled guests and the necessity of his person at the manse, he would teach the little fucker to suck his prick. He wiped his cock on the bed cover and began to dress, kicking Tillie aside when she sought him, thusly proving that she wanted to be fucked even if she pained over her daughter's initiation to a lusty man's penis.

He thought about Joseph Fedren, raking leaves and shearing sward. A strong back and weak mind and no eyes to see nor a cock to turn the seeing into pleasure. At the cottage door, he winked lasciviously at Tillie and went out.

Tillie stood, facing the bed upon which Mary lay motionless. Her feet were far apart, her body was crouched in a fierce double curve that pushed her throbbing cunt out and allowed her tits to rest on her back tilted torso. Mary was hurt, perhaps vitally but before she could help her daughter, she had to release the torturing tensions. Molding her belly with one hand, Tillie inserted the handle of Joseph's hand spade into her broadly opened cunt and sent the sweat polished hickory in as far as it would go. She held the tool so that at the end of every plunge, her thumb knuckle beat against the swollen ridge of her clitoris. She wept, she twisted and humped and her buttocks flopped with the fury of her undulations. She had cum quickly, disappointingly and resumed her masturbation with fresh frenzy. All the while, her eyes burned hotly into the small bottom so brutally assaulted by Jan Macklin. She remembered the insertion, the lusting, the screams of agony which could not have been pure agony from Mary. She smelled Jan's sweat, the funkiness of his cock, and the unsubtle odor as the inner rounds of Mary's ass showed churned brown at each coursing. When she had cum a second time, Tillie sagged to her knees and wept genuine tears for the devastation of her daughter. And it would never stop. Tillie knew Mary very well; she possessed the tingling body and the temperament and the love of sexual pain that had reduced her mother to a pulsating dummy for any virile man's lust. She tried to ignore the ugly hate for Mary that rose when she remembered how enamoured of Mary's baby body the cruel Jan had been. She had long known he fucked most of the women on the estate, but that was elsewhere. Tillie was jealous of her daughter.

"My poor baby!" she gasped and fell to the bed, her heart gushing with sympathy and love.

"M-mama?"

"Yes, my darling. I am right here. Do you hurt badly?"

"I think so. Is he gone?"

"Yes, Mary, he has gone, the mother-sucking beast!"

"We have done wrong, haven't we?"

Tillie didn't answer. She lay cuddling her daughter, petting her bruised flesh and trying not to think of what she had become. There had been one fragment of a minute when she had known the answer. With Jan's huge cock solidly imbedded in Mary's rectum, she, Tillie Fedren, mother, woman, wife of a good man, could have picked up Jan's own game gun and blown his backbone in two. No man, no court in all the land would have blamed her; Jan Macklin was of no better class than herself, and they would have buried him in a dastard's grave. She hadn't done it for reasons she could not stand to think about.

Presently, she got up and fired some water, and white Mary lay whimpering, Tillie cleansed and salved her daughter's wounded bum. She hated herself for the memories she recalled, and for the strange delight she took in fingering and petting the flaccid anus. She despised herself for wanting to put her mouth to Mary's inflamed cunt and easing the girl's pain with violent mouth caress. Her own tensions eased when Mary asked, "Mama, are all men so cruel, so bestial?"

As if committed by rote, Tillie explained about all the fierce things a brutal, lusty man could do to a tender, passionate woman and when Mary's eyes became round and wet with fright, she could not stop her recitation. She even added some things she had long dreamed of and which no man had yet thought to do to her.

"They delight in seeing blood, particularly if it is caused by their ramming cocks, my baby. They seek to tear a woman and perforate her innards, to make her scream upon their rampant vanities and suffer the tortures of the damned. They claw your thighs and grind their teeth into your tits, or when yours grow forth and they wallow in the filth their ruthless cocks churn out of your improper place. They ravage the very young, exulting in the misadjustment of a virgin child and a full-grown male and they adore thrusting their pricks into places not meant for receiving their foul jism."

"Even daddy?" Mary asked, breathlessly.

Tillie shrugged. "Your father is a farm hand, a beast of burden without a yolk! I love him dearly but he is as puny as Jan Macklin is a brute! Ah, Mary, we must now become very close, closer than we have been all these growing years of yours. I love you very much and you must love me because God created us with pits of sin and violence and gave us not the will nor the strength to repel the ever rampant pricks that men adore for their power of devastation."

"Yes, Mama. I love you very much," Mary insisted, kissing her naked mother's cheek. "I feel better, now."

"Do you like being naked with me, my darling?"

"Oh? Well, yes, it is very warm and cozy. Your fingers soothe me, Mama. Could you touch a little higher? It would feel quite good, I'm sure! And I could touch you if you wanted me to."

"Of course, my darling. Like all women, your mama

35

loves gentleness and affection. Oh, your fingers are so—so small!"

"Your wetness smells very good, Mama," Mary murmured. "And I dream of the day my parts are haired like yours! Oh! There, Mama?"

"He may come again tomorrow and you should be enlarged, I think, so his organ does not make you faint as it did today."

"If only he did not go so far," Mary murmured.

"It is a woman's lot to be large enough, dear Mary. A man can not be expected to understand the end of acceptance."

"You are so wise, Mama."

Tillie shivered and let her soothing kisses move lower and lower on her daughter's quivering body. Joseph could not get back to the cottage a moment before sundown.

three

The first post chaise arrived at the Tensington gate at dusk. Jan, wearing his finest jacket and his narrow-brimmed gaming hat, ignored the driver and touched his forehead to the handsome fop who peered through the carriage window, then swept the other trio, who were females, with a flick of his eyes. As a gesture of welcome, his whip went out and touched the flank of a team horse, sending the speedy carriage into the Manse drive at full tilt.

A second carriage arrived before the dust of the first had properly settled, and within an hour three more had been sent on to the postern. Lights had appeared at many second floor windows as the guests were shown to their respective quarters by the inside servants. Jan cruised the manse yard making sure that the oil lamps at the terraces were burning with a minimum of smoke. He merely glanced toward the stables where three of the coaches, not hired carriers, were being put up. The remaining two had headed back for London after the drivers had been paid and given a pot of wine.

In the dark, Jan strolled about the grounds listening at various points to small bursts of feminine laughter and occasionally, a more robust merriment. They a score of happy ones, he decided. The half-count he·had kept told him there were a few more women than men, which to Jan was a proper division of interests. When he knew dinner had been served, Jan stopped at the kitchen entry and Belle brought him thick roast beef and hot tea, laced with brandy.

"And this is a rum crowd, I'll tell you, Jan!" she giggled. "Ah, the gentry are so handsome and so well garbed! And the ladies, if that is their title, you wouldn't believe! They drink much and laugh a great deal and they do not mind to be pinched and felt of. It is to be a whoring weekend, you may be sure!"

Jan chewed strongly and did not reply. His place in Tensington was singular. He was not, of course, of the gentry, but neither was he a servant. He also knew the folly of expressing opinions to the like of Belle. But he was interested in what she had said. He privately knew that in the late hours of a merry night, some London fluffies wearied of their slim, half-masculine companions and bruited about in search of more spirited adventure. He·felt of Belle's bottom and wiped his greasy fingers on her skirt in so doing. Then he continued his slow tour, stopping when he came to flickering oil pots in case some bright-eyed guest were already scanning the manse yard for a cure to boredom. He was a patient man.

He could have foretold within minutes the time when the party moved to the second floor and the alcoves reached by half flights required by the architecture of the ancient house. There were not only the bedchambers, but the gaming rooms and the large second parlour which had once been a library and music center. There were three stairways to this more intimate level, and two could be shut off by the turn of a key, leaving only the huge winding staircase from the lower hallway. A word from Frederick II would restrict that stairway to Gibson who carried the keys to the wine cellar, and perhaps to Lydia, who saw to the linens and personal services of the guests.

Jan fondled the butt of his whip and searched the yards with keen eyes; Frederick would neither tolerate the curious nor the criminally inspired, and though the word had not been spoken, Jan knew that he guarded to keep frightened or replused guests from leaving as well as from being disturbed.

Marlene was apprehensive, nearly frightened. Ostensibly, she was the guest of honor, being the current light of the London stage. Invitation to the huge Tensington Manse had excited her, especially since Malcomb had tendered the invitation from Frederick Tensington II and garnished the matter with the names of five or six of London's most eligible bachelors. She had felt secure because all were gentry and of the ladies mentioned, two or three were from the best families in England. But as Marlne watched Malcomb Fageol, her escort, press furiously to the half displaced bodice of Anne Grange, his kisses raining on the warm expanse of her throat and face while his hands moved firmly over her back and bottom, she sensed the underlying pulse of the approaching weekend. Nor was Malcomb alone in his pursuit of the ladies. Others of the men were even more bold. Already, the grouping had dispersed and through this elegant room and the adjoining chambers, couples had formed in close whisperings, excited gigglings and an obvious exchange of personal contact.

Then Frederick Tensington was back, presenting her with another goblet of the fine strong brandy. He sat beside her on the divan, turning to raise his glass, his lean thigh pressing firmly to her trembling limb under the expensive gown.

"To the most beautiful lady who has ever graced Tensington!" he said, smiling broadly. "May your London success swell until the world grovels at your pretty feet, dear Marlene!"

"How kind," she murmured and tasted the brandy which she did not want. Her fourth or fifth, she remembered. And before that, dinner wines and very rich food. "Your estate is beautiful, Frederick. The house is magnificent, nearly a castle. Do you have affairs here often?"

Again he smiled. "Yes, because my grounds need constant supervision and I am not able to get down to London as often as I should like. And my London friends seem to enjoy a respite from the hustle and the crush of London."

"They all seem to—to be having a wonderful time,"

Marlene ventured, her comment being inspired by seeing a tall dark man crowding over a pretty redhaired girl with a more than an insistent thigh. Then she thought she sensed a small humming in her host's throat, as if he were mentally elsewhere, or at least occupied with distant thoughts. "I think I am very tired," she said. "Would I be impolite were I to retire, Frederick? It has been a strenuous past week in London and the three hour journey here has wearied me. And Malcomb seems to be pleasantly occupied! Would you excuse me?"

"But of course! And I shall escort you to your chamber. It is acceptable, is it not?"

"It is beautiful, so nicely done and in perfect taste!"

He stood and extended his arm. Marlene rose and took his proffered support. Her eyes flicked the others in the room. No one seemed to pay any attention to her, nor to the host. As he led her to the hallway that wound through the many rooms, she felt the apprehension return. He matched his step to hers, his body very close, his breath a flame of brandy fumes adding heat to her own natural flush. When they arrived at the door of her assigned room, he opened it and handed her it. When she turned to say good-night, he was also in the room, his square back to the closed door.

"Oh!" she gasped.

He advanced and before she could gather her brandy-scattered wits, his arms clamped around her and his mouth found hers with open-lipped, moist and deforming passion. She struggled, feeling the length of his vibrant body against hers as his hands became intimate on her back and lower.

"I am mad about you, Marlene, beautiful dream!"

he husked when she managed to turn her face from his ardent kiss. "You are everything Malcomb said you would be! I adore you!"

"Let me f-free, this instant!" she demanded. He locked his hands at her back and let her arch back. Instantly, she felt the hard bulge in his excellently tailored trousers. "Oh, no, no!" she panted. "Let me go, Frederick Tensington, let me go!"

"Ah, spirit, as Malcomb promised! He knows I like a woman who pretends to resist my charms! Fight me, Marlene, strike at me and cry out! It will make the moment of my passion a thing divine!"

"You—you beast!" Marlene screamed, and the sudden light in his eyes galvanized her into furious struggling, fists beating to his chest, feet kicking. His laughter sent chills of fear through her virgin body. This was not a mild struggle in a private supper room, nor a demure resistance in a hansom cab. Frederick seemed a devil, strong, ruthless and terrifying. The elegant room was a cell, and it was buried in a huge stone structure now populated by men and women of unspeakable evil. Suddenly she wrenched strongly and he seemed to let her go. But as she flailed back, his hand caught in the stylishly low bodice and her gown ripped from breast to thigh. He laughed brashly and with a final jerk, left her standing only in her undergarments. She tried to cover the up-bulge of her full tits and the dark shadow of her pubic hair under the French lingerie. She jerked a backward step, eyes wide to the point of burning. He was removing his fine coat. Then he rolled his laced cuffs and slipped his cravat.

"No, no!" she breathed. "No! I am a virgin, untouched!"

"I know," he said through half-clenched teeth. "That is the only kind Malcomb brings to me."

Then he unwound his silken cummerbund. He folded it two times and twisted it until it formed a solid bit of maroon rope which he again folded and gripped, like a limber club of ominous weight. As he advanced she retreated, and when her back was to the wall, her spread fingers covering terror-drawn face, he struck her with the silken twist across the belly. Marlene screeched, less hurt than shocked. He hit her again across the tits, causing a fierce pain. Again alongside the head, spinning her. She fell to the bed, curled, clutching herself in abject terror. The blows rained over her, from head to toe, pummeling her at back and bottom, only slightly protected by her corset. She wept, sobbed mightily, and her mind seemed unable to function. She couldn't decide if the thudding cummerbund was really hurting her or if her mind created pain from her mental anguish.

Finally, the blows came sparingly, then not at all. She dared not move, dared not face the man she believed to be totally insane. She cringed inwardly but lay motionless. Then she felt his hands at her back, fumbling with the corset ties. She writhed and tried to roll. A lean knee smashed into her back and forced her to her belly, unable to do more than squirm and twist. She felt the release as her corset was loosened, then shame made her wail with agony as he jerked her silk panties down. Marlene tried desperately to free herself and the thudding cummerbund returned, now concentrating on her naked bottom. It beat her nates up, then down, then in between, each blow causing her to jerk and flinch. Her tits, now freed of the corset constriction, splayed under her rolling shoulders and ached with bruising.

"Oh God, oh God, strike him dead!" she pleaded and in return, Frederick's laughter was low and hideous. Abruptly, Marlene was too tired and too devastated to struggle more. She lay, her body quivering under the unreasonable cruelty, her mind detached from even fear.

———————————

Frederick dropped the cummerbund club and slowly stripped himself, his eyes devouring the delicate under-curves of the actress's ass. Her cunt was a closely tucked delight of darker pink, peeking back at him between her twitching thighs. The cheeks of her ass were so round and full he could not see her anus, but he visioned it, a tight, untrammeled rose awaiting his plucking. She seemed to have fainted but he read her immobility as defeat.

Naked now, he stood stroking his long, lean penis, fingering the foreskin back so the conical head jerked up in firm readiness. He wanted her naked so he half-knelt and began to roll her out of the flopping corset. He unsnapped her stocking clips, and bared her splen-did body. His breath hastened at sight of her full rolling tits and he now looked hotly at the other extremity of her cunt. It was plump and dry and the lip texture was softly rough and much darker than the surrounding skin, shining through the thickly grown pubic hair. With her clothes removed, he contemplated the perfect body, his prick swelling even more as he imagined what he might do. Then he looked at her face and to his surprise, and pleasure, Marlene was looking at him through narrowly slitted eyes. Impulsively, he bent and kissed her tit tips, letting his tongue punctuate the caresses with darting adoration.

"You will be divine, my darling, and I shall thrill your exquisite body until your senses depart!" he promised. "Do you like my prick, dear Marlene?"

Turning he stroked it out and back several times, aiming the fish-shaped head directly at her face. Slowly, as if in mortal pain, her head turned to the opposite wall. Frederick laughed softly. He had beaten her into complete surrender, now he would fuck her into screaming ecstasy. But there was a long, delicious night ahead and he had no intention of spending his passion hurriedly.

Suddenly, his hand shot down and his fingers grasped the soft layer of flesh lying over her belly. She screamed and he gripped tightly, drawing her hips up. Her legs went out, kicking for support on the bed and she wailed as she tried to lift herself to ease the nearly tearing of her skin. Frederick closed down upon her spraddled crotch and his mouth went to her quaking cunt with open lips and parted teeth. He bit deeply, barely failing to draw blood. The acrid flavor of her private part made ripples of joy run through him. He released the bite and his grip and as her hips settled down to the bed, he began to lick and nibble in the delightful organ. His tongue found her clitoris, then pushed down to probe and slightly perforated membrane of her maidenhead. He tried to thrust his tongue into the natural orifice and did, feeling the soft tissues stretch under his assault. Marlene was squirming and struggling, but his weight held her down, and now his hands went out to keep her strong thighs apart so he could work his lust in her quim. He was pleased by the quick swelling of her clitoral bud; his pursed lips sucked at it while his avid tongue taught the sensitive nubbin the nature of its creation. It was a thing he knew no woman could stand, no matter her rage, her fear or her humiliation. And after a few moments, he sensed the slackening of her resistance, the softening of her muscular tension. He moved, lifting one leg up to straddle her chest. His cock dropped to the heat of the valley between her tits. He visioned her first reactions; disgust at the exposure of his naked ass in her face, revulsion at the hairy hang of his large balls, and then, weird fascination as her eyes followed the length of his prick to its resting on her own flesh. He flexed his cock, making it bounce. His tongue settled to slow, wandering coursing over her widely opened quim. He let his saliva flow over her hot flesh and dribbled to the bottom corner of the delightful shape to soak into the hair of her down-curves. He also could not resist the small urging of his own hips, his glans rubbing her skin with exquisite irritation. And when her hips did a certain small movement that met his laving tongue, he knew he had conquered Marlene de la Sage. A moment later, one of her shaking hands came to lay around the outside of his strained thighs. He pursued his assault, turning her first subtle response into a lowly increasing roll. His hands went under and cupped the cheeks of her ass, adding the pressure of his palms and fingers to the excruciating caress of his tongue. When she groaned and whimpered, "Oh God!" he again sent her into a screaming frenzy with his swift bite. Her fists beat at his bare bottom, her wails were hot gusts on his swinging balls. And as before, he suddenly ceased his torture to resume the subtle sucking and licking. Her gasp of relief was loud, and the return of her hip undulations was almost instantaneous. He was about to leave her properly suspended in near passion when he felt her fingers at his cock. He flattened his back, which moved his prick closer to her eyes. She pressed the shaft, then began to test the mobility of the skin. Other fingers fluttered at his ass, probing the soft places between the muscular knots. She cupped his balls and explored the rubbery weight of his scrotum. And the hand to his prick became possessive, nearly frigging. Then she simply held him, her soft moans vibrating in her throat. Frederick intensified his mouth, and her hips beat up in sudden surrender. His tongue again slipped down and entered the virginal orifice, and as she shuddered in gentle cum, his taste buds tingled with the ooze of her inwardly constricted vagina. He straightened up and as her body slowed in its ecstatic writhing, he thrust two long fingers into her vaginal membrane and ripped it with a ruthless jerk.

Her screams were shrill. He climbed to the floor and stood grinning and fondling his prick while she rolled and tossed, her legs drawn up, her hands closed over her cunt in protective agony. While she suffered, he picked up the cummerbund, reestablished its twisted firmness, then began to beat the bended bottom with measured thuds. His cock jerked up, swayed, swelled and began to throb with significant warning. Frederick beat on and after a few seconds, his prick spewed its load out in needle-sharp darts that struck Marlene's back and ran in gray-white trickles to the bed. His cum over her anguished body was long and exquisite. When his prick ceased spurting and sagged slightly for the last feeble dribbling, Frederick wiped his cock on her thin silk panties and sat down across the room from the bed, slouched easily, his eyes on her gradually increasing calm.

Marlene came to one elbow, her other hand pressing a corner of the coverlet to her slightly bleeding cunt. She stared around the room as if she had never seen it before. She looked at Frederick, his long naked body a relaxed obscenity in the heavy chair. His cock hung out from his hairy groin in a fearsome arc, the foreskin well back so the vicious head seemed very large.

"You have had your will," she said. "Leave me now!"

"But my dear Marlene! We have but lightly tasted the dear nectar of love! No matter how sweet you imagine your initiation to have been, I assure you of ecstasies beyond compare once you release your unnatural reticence. Did you enjoy your cum, my sweet?"

"You raped me," she said, irrelevantly, stupidly, she thought.

"A proper thrill for a virgin of twenty-three, was it not?"

She dropped back, panic-stricken by the unreasonable thoughts that swirled in her brain. "Will I have a child by you, Frederick?"

His laughter hurt more than her cunt. "But certainly it would be a marvel, born of Tensington saliva! Of course not, you silly goose! Nor will you from me! Several noted physicians have told me that I am, irrevocably, the last of the Tensingtons. My balls are un-virile, though they produce the gustiest jism in central England!"

Marlene bit her lip, somehow feeling that he was a worst beast than she had thought. Her training had been that a woman properly loved should produce a baby. That she wasn't sure of what being properly loved consisted of was due a bit to her moments of blackness during the session of alternating pain and ecstasy. Her body felt strange, not bruised from his beating but oddly sensitive, as if a hand or a more heinous touch would turn her flesh to fire. She closed her eyes, trying desperately not to cry as wave after wave of hate and humiliation flushed her skin. When she opened her eyes, he was standing at her side, the gigantic finger of white and scarlet hanging over her face. There was a drop of viscid fluid at the tiny fishmouth of the end. The long column throbbed, rising and thickening and distending at each pulsation. Shamefully, she remembered the exciting moment when she had seemed compelled to feel of it and the ugly sack hanging there in hairy weight. Even now, she could not recognize herself as she stared at the blossoming organ; he had beaten her, defiled her and laughed at her innocence, yet she had deep stirrings of vague description as she inhaled the musky odor of his body. Suddenly, she screamed as total hysteria gripped her.

Instantly, his hand closed in her hair and a soft firm animal seemed trying to crawl down her throat. Held, she opened her eyes and nearly choked, with stunned mind and a well-filled mouth. His organ was pulsing hotly on her tongue, she tried to swallow and the warm column, surprisingly layered with soft flesh, moved in and out of her lips with firm intent. She thought of biting fiercely; another thought of blood and violence made her shudder. She stared at the way Frederick's belly moved, the acrid taste of his organ was nasty but intriguing. Her saliva gathered rapidly and she had to swallow or choke. His hand in her hair twisted brutally and she let his prick pump the saliva out around its coursing girth. Held so, Marlene seemed unable to do but what he desired her to do. She tried to block the thrust with her tongue and an unbelievable quiver went down her spine as she learned the shape of the monster in her mouth. Her breath rushed harshly through her flared nostrils. In defence of a hard thud at the back of her throat, she raised a hand and pressed his belly, again shuddering at the feel of haired flesh, working as he moved his hips in lewd undulations.

"Ah," he breathed above her. "My innocent darling sucks my prick like a devotee! Tongue it, Marlene, and find your pleasure in understanding my delight!"

Her hand still holding the coverlet between her legs seemed incapable of remaining still. She moaned deep in her throat as she felt herself sinking in the mire of sensualism. What she did was lewd and sinful, but as the cock in her mouth thickened and throbbed, she felt impelled to urge it with tongue and lip pressure. Her hand no longer pressed him away. It had dropped to hold the thick shaft, permitting her to roll her head and change the in and out of the sweet knob. She abruptly realized he was no longer holding her head with his painful grip in her hair. She flushed as she ignored the chance to spit him free and bury her face in the pillow behind. To what this obscene moment could lead, she had no idea, but for the instant, she had not the will to care. Then he did a most impolite and revolting thing. At first she thought he had urinated in her mouth, but the fluid came in hard spurts, striking her throat, lying heavily on her tongue and filling her mouth with slime. She coughed and he let her draw away. She coughed and swallowed, then spit the rest of the thick, musky fluid to the bed. His prick spit also, the hot drops pecking at her forehead. When she tried to wipe it away, it only smeared. Gagging, panting, she turned away and fell face to the bed in forlorn revulsion. His laughter was like another beating.

She had a moment then to analyze her thoughts. Virginal, innocent of sexual adventures, she yet had been exposed to the brasher, less successful people in the London theater. She knew many words of a vile nature, although many of them were obscure in their correct meaning. There was now no doubt in her harassed mind about what anyone meant when they called an unpopular member of the cast a cocksucker. A cum, at least on a man's part, was also obvious. And the ugly taste, the clinging slime was jism. The screaming terror in her mind was not for knowledge, it was for the deep inner excitement experiencing the horrors had created. Nor could she ignore the fact that all of the sweet promises she had grown up anticipating when she finally fell in love were being enacted in pure venality. Then her nearly exhausted sense of survival made her seek a new grip on her mind and nerves. Her cunt was slightly sore but other than that, she was unhurt except as she thought about things. A wheel departed from the post chaise from London would have done her infinitely more damage.

Then his weight was on the bed and she sensed he was gathering over her. She opened one eye and saw his hand very close, palm down on the bed. Then she felt his cock, unlike any other touch in her memory, nudging at her bottom. It jabbed gently, then with more firmness and more accuracy. She jerked, opened her eyes fully and turned her head to look directly up into his lust-taut face.

51

"What—what do you do?" she gasped.

"Lie quietly and the answer to your question will burst upon your senses like a bonquet from heaven!"

"No, no more! Oh, I can stand no more!"

But the insistent cock was there, pushing from behind into her wounded quim. She tried to evade it and did not know how. His legs seemed to have hers secured in folding. She felt the edges, already torn, being pressed and to ease the fresh pains, she lefted her uppermost thigh which reduced the agony, but brought fresh fright. The prick seemed to screw itself inward, spreading her unmercilessly, filling her with aches. Her fists clenched; she would not succumb. She could feel it very deep now, surging slowly, accompanied by a multitude of startling sensations.

His hairy belly was rough on her hip, his balls knocked at the lower cheek of her ass. In her mind, his cock was as huge as a tree trunk and as long. She lay quietly, waiting for the bonquet from heaven and when it came, she twitched in shock. He was sliding forward and back on her, his prick was coursing in her body with fiery power, and at the beginning of each pressure, his rock-hard organ touched the still irritated place at the front of her quim. She moaned in misery as the bouquet became sweeter than the pain.

She knew then that she was being fucked and that his first rape of her had been some finesse of the sensual. He had sucked her cunt to its first lust-inspired cum, just as she had sucked his cock to spurting a few minutes later. Weeping, Marlene began to lend her physical self to the demanding pistoning in her belly. It was excruciatingly good, frightening, delectable and terrorizing all at once. Her tits ached with pulsing and her arms and hands wanted to flail and beat the bed. Once, she wanted even to turn and clutch up at the straining body above hers, to haul him close and thusly deeper and to mash her lips to the hotness of his skin. Instead, she just let her body do all the movements it seemed to need in order to accomplish the beautiful promise each thrust he made sent to her brain.

The moment she lent herself to the cruel intrusion, the play changed themes. Despite the hate and revulsion she felt for Frederick Tensington, the thing they did together became vital, excruciatingly wonderful. She could no longer pretend indifference or listlessness and her panting and squirming and back-humping became as violent as his. She didn't quite understand the physical and mental peak she sought but when she climbed to it, the summit was divine and she shuddered and groaned with orgasm so extreme it left her whimpering and nerveless.

Later, he fucked her again but the glory had gone with the first rape of her womb and she lay under him, hating and despising. She had orgasm again because she did not know how not to, and her quim was so tender and irritated she could not control herself.

Eventually, he left her room and Marlene lay, devastated, forlorn and humiliated. Her body was a mass of soft bruises and filth. In the bath chamber she urinated with blood flecks and vomited until her belly ached with strain. Finally, she fell to the soiled bed and dozed fitfully until exhaustion fully had its way.

four

The sun seemed well up when she awakened in the morning and for a moment, Marlene lay in the pleasant stupor following a deep sleep. Then she remembered and a gust of grief brought tears to her eyes. She felt every muscle and nerve in her body as if each were a protesting fibre in her fingers. A few seconds later the door to her room opened and a pretty plump girl bearing a tray of steaming tea and crumpets entered. Her smile was bright.

"I am Lydia, Miss Marlene," she said with a curtsey. "I saw you once in London, from the third tier, of course. You are my very favorite actress! How are you feeling this morning, Miss Marlene?"

"W-well enough. Thank you, Lydia."

The maid poured the tea and arranged the tray at the bedside. Then she busied herself with straightening the bed and tidying the room. She seemed not to notice that Marlene sipped the tea, wanting desperately to question the girl about the other guests, and perhaps, to enlist her help in escaping the foul estate.

"Master Tensington," she began. "Is he about as yet?"

Lydia laughed and winked lasciviously. "No, indeed, Miss Marlene! I think you done him in proper, last night!"

"I—I did him in?" Marlene gasped. "What do you mean—?"

Again the lewd wink. "He was like a dead man when I put him to bed last night!"

Marlene held onto her hysteria. "The other guests?"

"Oh, some are riding in the hedgerows. Some are about, having breakfast or just tea, and three or four of the ladies are together laughing and primping for the day. When you have had your tea, should I bring water for your bath, Miss Marlene?"

"Yes. That would be delightful, Lydia. But first. I must get back to London today. I have remembered an appointment with the manager of my next play. Now I would not like to seem an unappreciative guest and I shall try to return before nightfall. I wonder if it is possible for you to contact some one at the stables to arrange for my quick trip to London? Could you do that?"

Lydia's eyes widened. "But Miss Marlene, you need only to mention your desires to Master Tensington and all will be taken care of! I will speak to him immediately he awakens and—"

Marlene sat up and smiled beguilingly. "No, no, Lydia, you do not understand! I would like these arrangements to be very circumspect. A secret, perhaps between you and I and the carriage man. Would you not like to help me a bit, Lydia?"

"Oh yes, Miss Marlene! It would be an honor to assist you in anything you might name! Well, then. I will bring your bath water and while you bathe, I will confide in Jan Macklin. He is the one to see—his position as groundsman puts him in control of the stable men and I assure you, he can be most discreet! No one but Master Tensington may question his authority—and he will be pleased to serve such a beautiful and famous lady as yourself!"

"You are a dear," Marlene said then. "As it will be only a quick trip, I need not pack my things. I shall be gone before the other guests know I have departed and I shall return before they can become alarmed. Now, there's a dear, and you shall have a pound note all for your very own, Lydia!"

"Oh, Lordy me!" Lydia gasped, then came out of her near swoon and went off for the bath water.

Hope of escape enlivened Marlene. She slipped out of bed, winced at the peculiar stiffness of her hip joints, then surveyed her nakedness in the big mirror. It was odd, she thought, that a woman could be so completely destroyed and yet show no marks of destruction. She tested her tits. They were slightly bruised but no more so than were her buttocks and thighs. She flushed heavily as she remembered the ruthless manner of the bruising, then a moment of exquisite memory came as she recalled the blazing ecstasies that had accompanied her destruction. She flushed further as she recalled how

Lydia had winked and remarked Frederick's exhaustion when the maid, brash country wench, had put him to bed.

But then, in a few minutes, an hour, perhaps, she would be away from this evil manse and its rapacious master. Once in London, she was safe, and the world need never know of her night of terror.

It was an interesting development but one Jan Macklin had no intention of furthering until he had conferred with Frederick Benning Tensington II. Particularly since the stupid Lydia had, with endless giggling, told him that the famous Miss Marlene had, the previous night, stripped the master's balls and sent him to bed with a hump in his back. Knowing a few of his employer's habits as practised upon some of the more comely and willing wenches on the estate, Jan surmised that in Tensington's cups, he had belabored the actress and fucked her between lumpings. As a man who had little respect for a woman's mind and even less for her tempers over the length of a prick and the manner of its plunging, he regarded her excuse about a London appointment suddenly remembered as a wily attempt to escape Tensington's boisterous attentions.

Nor was Jan fooled by any pretense of gentlemen and ladies. He had slept shortly and had been awake when the three men and two exquisite fluffies had demanded mounts for a morning ride over the Tensington fields. He had noted the bouncing tits and the way the women's riding skirts had laid over obviously naked thighs and hips. He had heard a few remarks not common to the drawing rooms and there had been a positive lasciviousness to the laughter and carousing he had heard during his night of guard duty. This was a fucking party, pure and simple, and he was not going to jeopardize his comfortable job as Tensington groundskeeper because some fancy bitch wanted to back out of a handy arrangement.

But Jan was also an opportunist. His cock had twitched as Lydia had described the beauteous Miss Marlene. Privately, he considered all actresses strumpets, though he had never known one personally. She had agreed to the weekend at Tensington; she must have bargained on cock in endless parade. And because she did not like the length, girth and tendencies of the master's prick did not mean she would sulk at the services of a more virile man. He licked his lips. A little subtle fol-de-rol might charm the actress into spreading her ass to him, and once he'd cocked her quim, she'd take a dozen times the lumping she had disliked from Freddie II. His blood speeded as he thought of the beautiful and famous Marlene de la Sage, begging to suck his cock if he would only cease laying his whip to her.

But such a delight demanded time and planning. Jan went to the stable and picked a horse and a light, four-wheeled carriage. He told the stable boy to take it to his cottage, and secure it behind the backthorn thicket. Then he went to the manse and found Lydia. He told her precisely how the actress was to wend her way to his cottage and he threatened to skin Lydia's tits with a dull knife if she so much as breathed about the developing conspiracy.

When she arrived at the cottage, Marlene thought it attractive if small, and passed its gate in breathless haste. She was still marveling over how she had passed through the manse gardens, around some heavy shrubbery and to this nearly secluded cottage without having met a soul. And there, as Lydia had said it would be, was the thorny thicket. She even heard the restless snort of a standing horse. She hurried forward and around the black-green growths.

Hunkered on the ground by the sagging carriage was a very big man. He was shirtless and the rippling muscles of his broad back gleamed whitely in the sun. He was intently working on the hub of a carriage wheel and to her dismay, she saw that it belonged to her probable escape vehicle. "Oh!" she gasped.

He swung around to face her. He was undeniably handsome, and his half naked masculinity was impressive. He smiled and stood up, towering well above most of the men she remembered.

"Miss Marlene? I'm Jan Macklin. I am sorry but we are delayed by a cracked wheel which I will later use to break the back of the fool who ignored its weakness. Within the hour I will have it repaired, however. There is nothing else to do."

"Oh, Mister Macklin, I am in such a hurry! Is there not another carriage perhaps?"

He smiled again, engagingly, and shook his head. "But, miss, I am risking much as it is. To return this carriage and obtain another might well begin a circle of whispering that would reach the master's ears. Surely, half an hour or so—"

Marlene shuddered. Her eyes turned back toward the manse, expecting any moment to see a vengeful Frederick striding through the brush. Last night in lust

59

he had been cruel beyond her imagination. In anger, he would be a perfect demon.

"Do not fret, Miss Marlene," the big man said, obviously reading her concern. "I bid you rest in my cottage, a mean thing but inviolate. Come. I will make you tea and see that you are comfortable while I mend this abomination of the carriage maker's craft!"

He came forward, his hand on her arm was huge and strong and before she could protest, he was leading her back to the cottage gate. Even in the warm sun, she shivered because his closeness stirred some fears of the previous night, and he was bigger and handsomer than any leading man she had ever acted with. The interior of the cottage was as she expected it to be, neat, frugal and bereft of feminine touches. She sat in the chair he indicated, then watched him move to a cracked basin to wash before he made her tea.

"I—I am putting you to a great deal of trouble, Mister Macklin," she ventured. "I know you are a valuable asset to Tensington."

Again he turned a broad, pleasant smile. "What I do, I do well, Miss Marlene. I have agreed to aid you and it will be done. Even, I might add, if you were not the most beautiful and striking woman I have even seen! Do you take sugar with your tea?"

For a moment, she couldn't remember. He was standing now, his body a massive straightness, the upper portion intriguingly patterned with strong growth of sandy hair. Just above his breeches belt his deep navel indented the flatness of his torso. Because she still maintained images of Frederick's nakedness, her eyes dropped lower. Her mouth parted in slight shock as she saw the huge and obvious bulge of his genitals.

"S-sugar, I believe," she husked. "I—I feel a bit faint."

"Well now! That calls for something more virile than tea!" He moved to a cupboard and turned with a bottle in his hand. He plucked the cork free with a loud pop, then thrust it out to her. "Drink," he said in a different voice.

Marlene opened her mouth to protest his domineering command. She stared straight into his eyes and they were very blue and made of steel. The hand clasping the bottle seemed able to crush the dark glass. And the faint odor of the brandy mingled with the musky odor of his bare skin. She raised a quivering hand and took the bottle. In all of her life she had never drunk from a bottle. She placed the neck to her lips and swallowed lightly. Abruptly, he grasped the bottle and put his other hand to the back of her head. She gasped and nearly choked, eliciting another memory, then to keep from drowning, she swallowed and swallowed, the flaming liquid scalding her throat and stomach as he enforced her drinking. Finally, she could swallow no more and it gushed from the protesting corners of her mouth. He stepped back, laughing as she fought to regain her breath and her equilibrium. She wanted to vomit but couldn't. She tried to scream but her throat was coated with raw flame. When he raised the bottle and took a long, hard pull from it, her eyes stared at his muscular throat with strange fascination. He was a brute, a beast, she thought, then her hiccup jolted.

She started to rise; better to forsake escape from a gentleman than to court disaster at the hands of a clumsy country clod. A wave of dizziness set her back in the chair. His laughter seemed endless. His prick when he took it out and shook it before her eyes was the most frightening thing she had ever known. It was much longer and thicker than Frederick's and it jerked and throbbed as he held it well toward his groin and massaged it firmly. She had one flash of certainty; the groundskeeper of Tensington Estates would never select a carriage with a cracked wheel for a three hour trip to London. She was caught in a carnal trap from which there seemed no possible escape. The cock now stood at a slight upward tilt, and she could see the twin puffs of the underglans and the thick tube that ran the length of the organ to fade into erotic shadows made by deep brown hair and the wrinkled dangle of his scrotum. She waited.

"Now, that's better, my darling," he chuckled. "You will like it better as you try it. Another drink, woman," he said in the same commanding voice.

With nerveless fingers, she took the bottle and tipped it, swallowing as many times as she could before the fire choked her throat. At least, she thought, her teeth had not been smashed and the brandy might dull the anguish she anticipated. She belched, all resistance crushed. The cock was swelling even more. It loomed as a white and pink and blue-red monster, watching her with its one upright eye and breathing through invisible nostril. Her eyes followed it in hypnosis as he balanced on one leg and removed a boot, then duplicated the balancing and bending to remove the other. He then unbelted and dropped his breeches, exposing his mighty thighs and muscular buttocks. Without the half-shroud of his trousers, his cock seemed a forearm in length. Marlene shivered with exterior chill but the brandy fire soon ended the quaver.

"You fool, you peasant fool!" she breathed. "Do you think you can get away with this abhorrent behavior? I'll have Master Tensington flay your filthy hide within your death's breath!"

"So? Then it behooves me to gain a stride before I slip back into your proposed hell, does it not, woman?"

She hadn't seen the whip, hanging from a peg by the door, but as he seized the thick butt and let the viciously plaited length slither out, she let free a cry of fear. Then she narrowed her eyes. The foul presentation of his naked lust was one thing, but to take the whip to her famous and important hide was another. No man would dare. She stood up, trying to control the stagger abruptly upon her.

"You insufferable clod!" she spat. "You have not the courage to do more than strut and threaten!"

The whip whistled and her bodice, caught at the high neck, ripped down as if sliced by a surgeon's knife. She felt only the barest smarting when the lashes had popped. She gasped and looked down at her nearly exposed tits. The lashes snapped again and the lace of her corset-lift flew through the air like gale-blown feathers. Marlene stared at him in disbelief, backing a step or two until the backs of her knees bumped the bed. She held up a palm. "No. No, no!"

"Remove your clothes, cunt," he said. "Strip, or I will cut these elegant silks from you, bit by bit, with small pieces of your pretty hide to lend a flavor to my pleasure. Undress, woman!"

The lashes popped in her upraised palm. Marlene screamed and pressed her palm to her mouth. Last night she had thought her fear to be ultimate; with nerveless fingers, she began to loosen and slip her clothes, utterly unable to think of anything but the sweetness of death. He stood, whip dangling, his other hand working the stocking-like skin of his gigantic prick. She dropped her head and fought each garment she wore. And when she was finally nude, she stood with her head down, her hands trying diligently to cover her sexual part. Suddenly, he stepped forward and swung the whip. It wrapped around her middle, tying her hands down. He jerked and she spun fully around, lost her footing and went to the floor at his feet.

She felt no new pain, only humiliation. When her eyes raised and perceived his cock, stiffened out just above her face, she knew exactly what he wanted. Her mouth filled with saliva and her spine tingled. He laid the whip over her back, shaking it so the plaiting irritated her skin. Eyes closed, Marlene opened her mouth and pushed forward until the huge, hot knob was caught solidly in her lips. The taste was similar, the form familiar in her mouth, and presently, his movements were the same that Frederick had so delighted in.

It had been too easy, Jan thought. But he had been right. Her protests had been false, her indignance an act. Even now, she wept as her lips milked his prick of its last dribbles of jism. Her tits seemed taut to bursting, the nipples out like the first berries of Summer. She angered him with her mock fright and mumbled revulsion, and he kicked her away to a huddle on the floor. It had been too easy so he decided to make it more difficult for her to succumb.

She fought him slightly as he tied her wrists together, but she didn't cry out and beg until he had lifted her so the rope could be pulled over the cross rafters of the roof. Then the pain of her wrists and the strain of her shoulder joints turned her protests into agonized sobs. Her toes dangled so she could barely relieve the weight of her voluptuous body. She was beautiful that way, he decided. Her torso thinned her tits rose and pushed outward in stress, and her thighs formed perfectly as she sought to reach the floor. He tipped her head and laughed into her tear-streaked face. Her slack mouth showed him the misty layer of his cum still coating her tongue. A second thought made him bind her mouth; if she screamed as he wanted her to do, the whole of Tensington would descend upon his cottage. Satisfied, he stepped back and let his whip whistle, to smack and welt but not to cut. His prick came up in swift response to the furious struggle of her body and the muffled agonies of her throat. There was almost as much pleasure for Jan in lacing her tits and belly and buttocks as she turned, with light pink lines as there might have been in cutting her to bleeding shreds. He spun her with a whip wrap, then turned her back. She kicked at him when he came close but quickly put her foot down to ease the stretching of her torturned body. Presently, his cock seemed unmanagable so he moved close behind her and squatted to send his pulsing organ up under the perfect cheeks of her ass. She bucked and twisted until he held her hips. Her grunt and buck as his prick went into her quim from behind made Jan's fever rise and flood his senses. Legs outstretched in awkward bracing, he fucked up into the clutching cunt and let her frantic writhings suffice for sweet response. When she seemed to still, he reached around and curled his hands to her inner thighs. As he lifted, easing her strained wrists and arms, her legs parted and he sent his prick in until his hairy groin was hard against her soft ass. He straighted up then, her writhing body hung on his completely buried prick and between his spreading hands. He fucked with animal indifference, and when his cum exploded, he drove it high and deep into the quaking sleeve. Only then did he realize that her legs had half wound back around his, and that her moans and grunts had changed in tone and tempo. He lifted her off his spent cock and let her dangle again but she had ceased her furious kicking and her useless twisting. Her feet were now well apart and her cunt was open and slightly swollen. He watched his cum ooze from the deep nest and run down her inner legs in slow, thick trickles. He flicked her tit tips with brutal fingers and laughed at the hate that shone from her eyes.

"Well now, I think we understand each other, do we not, my pretty? From now, you do not question my dare to do, shall we say?"

He loosened the rag around her mouth. She sucked in a huge breath, then spat at him like an angry snake. "You dog!" she hissed. "You demented fiend! Kill me then, I dare you to kill me!"

Which made Jan frown, not because he would have minded beating and fucking her to death but because he was suddenly faced with how this exquisite interlude could be terminated. The sun rays through the cottage window suggested noon, or there-abouts and he knew that he might well be needed around the manse. He had to either keep her in his control or let her go back and scream her agonies to the gentry. He let her hang and slowly dressed again. In an hour or two she would faint from exhaustion. Already, her shoulders were distorted as if the sockets had parted. Her burst of defiance was ended. Reluctant, he released the rafter rope and caught her as she collapsed in his arms. He left her wrists tied and laid her on his bed. Still not sure of what he should do, he found more rope and retied her, spread-eagled to the head and foot of the stout steds. Although her eyes were open, she showed no sign of protest or acceptance. He replaced the gag against her sudden return to defiance. Then he picked up his whip and left her, locking his door with the big brass key.

"I know not what to do, sir," Jan said to Frederick. "She came to my cottage, obviously drunk and raging with sexual fire. I tried to calm her and she leaped upon me like a wild anmial. I even obtained a light carriage from the stables and offered to return her to London if she could not act as a proper guest and lady. I tried to quiet her with tea and she promptly tore off her clothes and begged me to cod her, I beg your pardon."

"And you did, you villian!" Frederick snapped.

Jan shrugged. "I am but a man and she is very beautiful. But it did not end her frenzies. In her struggles, she may have been marred, sire, but I did only the best I could. In the end, I tied her to my bed and gagged her raging mouth. I have come directly to you, Master Tensington, for wisdom I do not possess. What are we to do with the woman, so that your guests will not be perturbed?"

"She is secure in your cottage, you say?"

"Yes, sir."

"She's been whipped and fucked and her belly fired by wine?"

Jan dropped his head in mock embarrassment. "Yes, sir."

"That one," Frederick mused, sipping his cordial. "She intrigues me greatly, Jan. Man to man does she impress you as a protesting nearly-virgin and a woman of righteous morals or does she strike you as a protesting whore who delights in every degradation a man may enforce, but it must be enforced! Answer after I assure you I believe nothing you have said, except that you have whipped her and codded her and now have her painfully bundled in your cottage!"

Jan grinned. "She is a woman of rare potential, sir!"

"Hand me your whip."

When Jan complied, Frederick laid it out before him, ruffling the butt to make the lashes wriggle on the flagstone. He pursed his lips and flicked the whip in speculation.

"I have never dared but I think I am about to. Keep her as you have her, Jan, until I have solidified the delightful images in my mind. Do you know of one among your secret conquests who can feed and care for her until I have made certain arrangements?"

"One, sir."

"And who is she who loves your cock so much she will enter into such a conspiracy?"

"I am sworn to secrecy, sir!"

"I know, villain. It is I who give you the power to swear secrecy and I hereby revoke the privilege! Who is she?"

"Tillie Fedren, wife of Joseph."

"Ah, that one! I have long noted her voluptuous body and flashing eyes! Hame upon you, Jan Macklin, for not sooner sharing your secrets! Well, bring her to our service and we will talk of her at a later time! How will you manage her husband and her daughter?"

"I will send Joseph to Watertown for certain implements needed in the fields. The daughter is quite comely and alert. With a tuck or two, one of Lydia's servant dresses would fit Mary and she could aid about the manse while your guests are here."

"By God, Jan, no wonder my father loved you unreasonably! I find your evil as great as mine and your cunning a thing of positive enjoyment! So be it. The girl may act as my private maid. Proceed."

Jan made his departure with mixed emotions. He had gotten out of a nasty spot with the beautiful London girl, but he didn't relish Mary in the chambers of Frederick Tensington. Mary had been Jan's private project and there were yet many delights about her slim young body he wanted very much to sample. But he was not a man to question Fate in any advantageous role.

five

Each time she had thought the last horror was the worst, a new fright had appeared to scatter her partially collected wits. He had returned with his whip and his rough hands, teasing her with threats of a further beating and fondling her outraged body with neither finesse nor care for her embarrassments. Finally, Jan Macklin had retied her hands and feet and bundled her in a coarse ill-smelling blanket. Unable to protest nor ask questions, Marlene had submitted to the second segment of his new treatment in ever-growing terror.

He had carried her from his cottage and hurled her bruisingly into some sort of cart. She had heard the snap

70

of his whip and the horse's snort of pain. The trip had been very long, and when the cart stopped, Jan had spoken to a woman.

"Here's the woman, Tillie. You mind her well as I have told you. Tricks or female connivances will get the hide stripped from your ass, I assure you. Now, help me get her into the house."

"Yes, Jan," came the dull, unenthusiastic response.

Carried into the house between them, Marlene had tried to find hope in the presence of another woman. When she was able to see, her hopes were shattered because Jan Macklin had again tied her hands and ankles to the head and foot of the stout bedsteads.

"This be Tillie Fedren," he said, nodding to the surprisingly handsome woman. "She'll take care of you until you're needed again!"

They had talked low between them for a minute or so, then with a last leer, Jan Macklin had left. Instantly, Tillie Fedren's expression and attitude changed. She removed the stiffing gag, smiled, and brought warm water and soft cloths. Warily at first, they had become acquainted and in desperation, Marlene had recited her maltreatment at the hands of Jan Macklin. Through this, the woman had nodded and sighed and looked very forlorn.

"You dare not struggle, Miss Marlene," Tillie finally said, bathing the subtle bruises and fine pink welts. "The power of Jan Macklin is invincible. He has controlled my body and soul for several years, and the part that hurts the worst is that I cannot now do without him! As for Master Tensington, he exists in a world he inherited from an evil father and his wealth and position is only questionable by a man of superior peerage.

71

"Could you—could you just untie one of my arms, Tillie?"

"I have done enough to remove your muffler, Miss Marlene! Ah, the full bite of Jan's whip! I bear some deep scars as a true memory of his rage. And I must think of my dear daughter and my fine husband whom I love very much, the both!"

"Your husband," Marlene murmured. "I can not conceive of your avowed love for him while you submit to the lust of another man! Is there no sanity of body and emotions, even as you submit to constant rape. I am appalled, Tillie!"

"Oh? When he hung you high and whipped you, then thrust his huge prick into your squirming body, what did your mind conjure?"

Marlene jerked. "I do not know, I cannot say!"

"You have not said, but I know him well. Was there either love or hate in your senses when he presented his prick to your mouth and laughed at your revulsion?"

"Please, Tillie!"

The plainly clad woman smiled, her eyes flashing with some unspoken emotion. She put a hand to Marlene's breast bone, then slowly moved it down and from side to side, petting the thick rolls of white flesh, then smoothing down over the tautly stretched abdomen. "And what do you think as I stroke you, Miss Marlene? Do you think of London and the next program, or of rain, or of the Summers you spent at the beaches? Do you recite prayers to yourself or hate me because I am not tied to a bed like yourself? I think not! There! Is that not a pleasant touch that has only to do with you and me?"

Marlene's eyes widened as she raised her head and

watched Tillie's unmanicured fingers roll into and pet her quim. She could think of nothing; she thought of hanging on Jan Macklin's cock, wracked with pain and frenzied by fear, cursing him for not caring that his monstrous prick was sending fires of ecstasy through her tortured body; she thought of her muffled pleas to fuck her more which to his lust-deafened ears seemed only to be further protest; she thought of lying quietly so these adept fingers would fire and build the gigantic delight that burst in her womb and made her feel like a woman. Tears of frustration left her eyes and she shamefully tightened her hips to rise to Tillie's touching.

"You see, Miss Marlene? There is a part of a woman that is detached from her mind. It is a hungry, eager, demanding part that will take and adore excitement without needing any emotional basis. It is the part that delights in the mere sight and feel of a man's prick, no matter the man. I've thought of it often and it seems to me God made woman a weak and wanting thing with no strength to resist abominations she knows will give her pleasure. Like what I do now! I have never touched a full grown cunt, except my own, in all my life before, but I am compelled to caress your lovely body by some force I cannot explain! And I can tell by your fast breath and the little things you do with your muscles that you enjoy it—nay, need it! Not because you need to be fucked because I know you've bloody-well had it in the best shape it comes in. Because you need and want and desire the wonderful sensation of living. Ah, I love your beautiful body, your soft moist quiff and the certainty that what I do is of great delight to you!"

Marlene turned her head away, clamping her teeth in determination to prove the lascivious woman a liar. She darednot give in, dared not become one of the strange and helpless creatures Tillie had described. But there were the fingers, parting her cunt lips, caressing the sensitive nubbin with knowing skill, and above all, Marlene's slow inner crumbling as her sense of rightness gave way to the constant sensuality she had endured for endless hours.

"No, Tillie, no, no!" she pleaded. "I hate you, I hate what you do to my helpless body! No, Tillie, Oh, my God!"

For Tillie had laughed shortly and leaned down, her full mouth suddenly pressed hotly to Marlene's cunt. The shock was furious, the darting tongue a hundred times more demanding than her fingers had been. Marlene squirmed and tried to bump Tillie's head away and each move she made doubled Tillie's intensity and reduced Marlene's desire to evade the darting delight. Moaning with rising passion, Marlene tried to console her tumultuous mind; last night, Frederick had also been so enamoured of her private part that he had sucked her into a reluctant cum. If she closed her eyes and suffered, there seemed no difference. Then she began to get that irrepressible goodness and her eyes popped open. Tillie was licking slowly now, her head nearly still, but she had loosed her dress and her hands were ecstatically molding and rolling her own huge tits. Marlene screamed and violently shifted her hips but it was too late. As she began to throb and jerk, she prayed for death rather than the label she would have to wear for responding to Tillie's lesbian act.

But as she laypanting, glowing and worshipping the relaxation Tillie's avid mouth had brought, Marlene remembered that empassioned philosophy the simple

74

country woman had expounded. A need and a desire apart from custom, theology or up-bringing, a furious seeking of the purely sensual, and thusly, the obscene. Her weary mind saw a man's prick, Jan Macklin's, huge and throbbing and lusting to ram itself into her mouth or her cunt. Even as she unconsciously cringed from the fantasy, she could see how the prick deformed and crowded her inner shapes, and she could smell his musk and remember the taste of his jism in her mouth. With a jerk of anguish, Marlene sobbed in agony and presently, Tillie covered her with a light blanket.

Mary giggled, then clapped her hand over her mouth in alarm. But they hadn't heard her above their own laughter and lewd grunting. She stood, half-wrapped in the heavy velvet that partially shrouded the entry to the terrace sitting room. There were five of them in the intriguing heap, three beautiful London ladies and two boisterous gentlemen. The lady who seemed to form the center of group was not quite naked. Her dress was drawn up to the waist and down from the top. Her spread legs showed Mary the closely cropped crotch into which another of the ladies was kissing and licking with all the frenzy she could muster. Her own bottom seemed perched upon long, slender legs, bare, and thoroughly penetrated by the amazingly long and slender cock of the young gentleman with the serious face. It shocked Mary a bit to realize his prick was coursing in the lady's bum, but she seemed to combine his foul fucking with her own hard licking and without any problem. The third lady was astraddle the center one's face, her half bare hips grinding and rolling with evident effect. In turn, this excited beauty was leaning forward so her mouth could be forefully fucked by the second gentleman.

Mary's giggle had been for the peculiar and somehow disconnected rhythms of the five, and a little bit for the strange tensions the naked and near-naked arms and legs and bellies gave her young body. A voyeuristic moment was not new to Mary; she had watched Jan fuck her mother many, many times, and she had also seen her mother slobbering and whimpering on the groundskeeper's cock. She herself, but a day or so ago, had been fucked, delightfully, if painfully. But in Mary's childish mind, fucking and sucking and mauling the nakedness of her mother had always been a serious thing, accompanied by Jan's gutteral meannesses, his whip and some agonized wails from her mother. This five seemed engulfed in merriment, trading quips Mary could not understand and laughing at sudden jerks or gasps of response. The man screwing hard into the lady bum-hole kept smacking her thighs and reaching out to squeeze her rather small tits. The man whose cock plunged in the other woman's mouth was constantly laughing and saying quick things to the others. But if it was different and exotic to Mary, it was also tremendously erotic; her body twisted in the ill-fitting uniform loaned by Lydia and she rubbed into her crotch with avid fingers. Part of the excitement was the unfevered manner of their play. No one seemed in the furious haste she had noted in Jan and her mother. They wriggled and humped and rested, to change their positions and continue as if more interested in exercising their flesh than accomplishing the thing Jan and her mother called cumming. Breathing heavily but with silence, Mary stared, and her mind said that what they all did to each other was a great deal of fun.

Then the group seemed to fall apart. The man fucking the bobbing bottom gave a groan and a short yell. He seemed determined to drive the woman over the heap and she raised her head from the humping crotch and shrieked. The man whose cock coursed in the hot lips fell forward, and with cries and laughter, the entire five collapsed into a pile of kicking legs and tumbling bodies. Mary drew closer into the curtain because any one of them could look up and see her there. She was so excited the thought of turning to run never occurred to her. When the hand closed on her shoulder, she nearly fainted with recall; she was a farmer's daughter, sent to the manse to serve, not to spy on the gentry and their ladies.

"Now, what have we here?" Frederick Tensington asked, his smile a crooked, unmerry thing. "A country maid, educating herself at the expense of her betters! I dare say it was a bit different than the butt pinching that goes on among school children, eh?"

"I—I am sorry, Master Tensington! But it was strange—"

Then they were all around her, laughing, reorganizing their clothes, making sharp remarks about her big eyes and ill-fitting gray dress. From intense excitement, Mary went nearly to tears.

"Well, having seen it, I wonder if she'd like some of it?"

"Oh, Malcomb!" one of the ladies said. "She's just a baby!"

Another, the one who had lain under them all, laughed. "Look who is defending little girls! You must

77

have started at half her age to get a cunt like yours at twenty-one!"

"A feel wouldn't hurt any," the other young man said. "Personally, I started with my maiden aunt and by the time I became aware of young girls, the village clods had wisked them all off to the vicar's altar!"

There was more, and Mary began to quiver with fear for their vulgar disregard of words and deeds. She looked up at Frederick Tensington, her face stiff with concern. "Sire, I think it would be best if I returned to the kitchen, or somewhere!"

"Yes," he said, his voice suddenly quite gentle. "But not the kitchen, Mary. Go to my quarters and tidy up, if you will."

"Oh, yes sire! At once!"

Behind her clumping heels, a London lady laughed. "Dear Frederick, I hope you have the sense to grease that pole of yours before she tidies it up!"

"Anne, dear, you have a dirty mind," Tensington replied.

"A clean ass and a dirty mind. What else is required?"

Mary wished she were back on the bank of the wash creek.

The pleasant, near-smile he had worn only a few minutes before was gone. He shut the door behind him with a frightening firmness. Mary still straightening the bed, looked at him doubtfully. No one on the estate had ever said Frederick Tensington II was a kind man, and she saw him now as a tall, forbidding and stern master. He moved toward her, his face becoming heavy with speculation as if she were exactly what she had been, a naughty girl. Mary shivered.

"I—I am sorry, Master Tensington," she murmured.

"Yes, I am sure you are," he said, sitting on the bed she had just tidied. "But sorry is not quite the point. You have been an impudent child and chastisement is required. Without some physical reminder that what you have done is wrong, there is little meaning to sorry, is there?"

"I guess so, sire."

"Come here, Mary!"

She took the two hesitant steps that put her close enough for him to seize her arm. Mary clung to her fright and did not whimper when he spun her around and forced her over his lap, her body bent in the proper position for the spanking she expected. Both her father and her mother had spanked her before; she hardly thought Master Tensington as muscular as her father nor as angry as her mother had sometimes been so she prepared to produce the proper amount of respectful tears and wailing. What she was not prepared for was the manner in which he folded the borrowed dress well up over her back and then jerked her bloomers down around her knees. She wriggled in embarrassment as the cool air emphasized her nakedness.

"Ah, now!" he said and his palm smacked smartly to her bottom. It did not seem a heavy blow but Mary gasped at the stinging. The second smack was different, as if he had started it low and hit forward at her nates. It made a pulling sensation in her crotch and Mary suddenly became very conscious of the fact that she was lying half naked across a man's lap. Again the smack and she squirmed with genuine pain. She squeezed her buttocks together, to fortify them against the next blow and to hide as much as she could of her private places. She then became aware of how his other hand was pressed to the bare small of her back, steadying her for his striking hand. After another pair of smart blows, she started to cry. Then the hand on her back became firmer and the striking palm became a warm, moving thing on her bottom. She felt the fingers pressing between her nates and under, then her little legs pushed apart in surprise as one of the probing fingers went into her quim.

"Oh, oh, sire!" she gasped in protest.

"And you seem not to be a virgin," he said as if adding this to her transgression. "Indeed, your cunt seems well opened for a child of your tender years. Have you been fucked, Mary Fedren?"

"I—I do not know of what you speak, sire!" she panted.

She dared not tell; his finger was pushing deep from behind and it was pleasant, if rude, and she could still remember the five humping, laughing and meshing people in the exciting pile. Her tears dried instantly and when his finger moved to press the good place, Mary giggled.

"Well, well!" Frederick Tensington exclaimed. His single finger in the small slit was immediately joined by another and Mary mewled in response. Instantly, she was swung around and pushed flat to the bed, her legs hanging over the edge at his side. His fingers pushed and searched in her little quim and she did a small lifting thing with her hips when he next touched the good place. Her head whirled, her tingling bottom added to the delight his fingers were stirring in her low belly. She was then startled by the abrupt weight of his body on hers. The fingers slipped away, she heard him grunt and his breath was hot on the back of her neck. A moment later, she felt a very big, very hot and strangely familiar finger pushing from back and under and she yelped as the intruder forced her small slit into round acceptance. As she had done with Jan, Mary kinked her bottom up to correct the way the penis entered her vagina, and it entered and entered, sending shivers of delight up her back.

Her body in his hands seemed so slim and small he could hardly believe his cock was thrust into her cunt as far as it was. Frederick's breath came in excited rushes. His thighs pressed to spread her legs and give him room to stroke and the tightness of her hole was so exquisite the sweat broke on his forehead. Further impact came from her giggles and gasps. Her little ass cheeks bumped up to his hastily bared groin and she wriggled with enthusiasm as he pumped. In brief flashes of thought, he decided he had been the victim of his own ignorance. She knew exactly how to fuck him back and her childish merriment told him she was enjoying every second of it. Suddenly, he did not want to simply fuck the little vixen. He wanted to explore and develop her sex, to delight in every possibility of her immature sexuality. He wanted to get rid of his own hurriedly parted clothes and get Mary out of the ugly maid's attire. He needed her naked, in his naked embrace, feeling and devouring her small charms with his eyes until his cock could wait no longer. He grunted and reared back, dragging his swollen organ from the small hot nest.

For a second after he was out of her, the tiny ass continued to bob and roll. He nearly had cum on her buttocks, so exciting was her avidity.

"Get up, Mary," he husked. "Take off your clothes."

"Y'yes, sire," she panted and scrambled to her feet, her eyes adhered to his waving and jogging prick as he removed his own garments. Her loosely fitted dress came up and over her head in a twinkling. She kicked down and out of her bloomers and slipped her under shirt up and away. Frederick stared at the slim form, hardly as thick as his thigh, smooth, firm and glowing with the fire of youth. Her little cunt was a mere slice in the small pad of flesh at the tip of her flat stomach. Her tits were thin mounds, barely discernible, but the pink tips were prominently outthrust. Frederick sat down on the bed and pulled her so she stood between his thighs, his cock up and kissing the flesh of her belly.

"You must tell me who has taught you to fuck, Mary," he said, running his hands over her waist and hips to cup the tiny cheeks of her ass.

"A man. A man in the field did it to me twice a few weeks ago," she said, not looking at him.

"What man?"

"I do not know his name. It was at the time of the second weeding in the young barley. Oh, sire, have I done something wrong?"

"Did you like it, Mary?"

"It hurt at first. But it was—was all right then!"

"Yes," he breathed. Then he turned her into one arm and lifted her quickly parted legs to his lap. His fingers plunged into the moist little cunt and he moved to find the tiny solid button of her clitoris. She moaned and her legs parted even more. He ran his fingers in and out, marveling at the tensions she generated around them. His cock jerked up and bounded against the cheeks of her ass and he hunched to repeat the soft contact. But it was her little quiff that intrigued him. His fingers had opened the outer lips and had dragged out the frayed inner lobes of her destroyed maidenhead. As he frigged her, she put one arm up and hooked her little hand over his shoulder which gave her bracing to meeting his plunging fingers with writhing hunches. He could feel her tremble, and her cunt constantly convulsed, milking his digits with unabashed eagerness. He wanted to fuck her then but he was hypnotized by her total response to his frigging and he decided to see if her undeveloped body were capable of orgasm. Her legs were waving, heels kicking, but as he increased the speed and intensity of his fingers, the slender limbs drew up and up until her small ass was thrust forward in sharp bending. He saw her little asshole, a mere dare pink blemish in the diminutive valley between her taut buttocks. By twisting his hand he could press the incipient tearose and he did, his cock swelling at the rubbery feel of the little anus. She seemed not to care, or even notice and he let the tip of his finger press until the tightly closed ringlet relaxed slightly. But his frigging was beginning to have its desired end; she was gasping and mewling and fluttering as if all control were gone. Frederick had never seen such a sensuous sight in his life; the swiftly rising passion of a child so small, and somewhat innocent was like the creation of a being or the death of one.

"Oh, oh, oh, sire!" she cried. "Oh, it is so—so good, so very g-good!"

He stilled his two fingers, letting the secret muscles

of her quaking cunt milk them in unrestrained cumming. Had his fascination for her physical contortions been any less, he would have had to fuck her instantly because his cock was throbbing in massive distress. He jerked his fingers from her quim and watched the few final clutching of the inner lips. A small froth appeared, and the odor of it wafted upward, sweet and female, giving Frederick a moment of pure need. He almost threw her around on the bed and plunged his mouth to the small delight. Her legs closed against his ears, but her clamp was not in protest. Almost instantly, she parted her thighs and hunched up to the darting tongue, tasting and exploring the small cavern. Frederick marveled at her quick rebound from her first cum; she fucked up to his face as his nibbling lips and inner licking proceeded and her panting moans were as eager as if it were her maiden flight into passion. His saliva overflowed and wetted her almost hairless crotch, trickling down to nest in the fundibular hollow of her anus. Frederick put a finger to the wet rose and thrust in, too excited to be gentle and too eager to be slow. Mary yelped but did not twist away. He turned and crooked his finger, delighting in the quick way the tight circlet relaxed as he plunged and felt of the inner tissues. Again his cock seemed about to leap from his groin and his balls rolled in anxious knotting but he was stilled by the fabulous sensations he was creating for her and for himself. His mouth completely covered the small cunt, and his tongue plunged like the stamen of a viscous flower, and from her asshole he could feel the coursing of his mouth-fucking. Lost in the fury of his perverted ecstacies, he did not feel her rising to a second cum until it was thumping in his mouth. She twisted and writhed, the tendons of her inner thighs standing out like velvet-covered ropes. Slowly, Frederick rose out of his trance, his eyes staring down at the little body slowly quieting from the sweet anguishes of naked lust. She was watching him, her eyes narrowed, her mouth slack in relaxing.

Then he felt his cum gathering and he fell over her, letting his rock-hard prick wedge into the wet little cunt. He curled his spine and shuddered delightfully as his prick went in, lubricated by his saliva and her oozing fluids. He thrust until she gave a small cry and raised her palms to his chest to stop him. He was in her very deep, he thought, because his balls knocked to her ass. He held and with a massive shudder, released his jism in furious spewing. Every pulse of the fiery discharge rippled as it passed the grip of her expanded cunt lips and as Frederick slowly churned his prick, he could feel the thick cream of his balls easing the constricted sleeve and soothing his tingling glans.

"Oh, sire, you hurt me so," Mary whispered. "I pray you do not push in so hard! I am in p-pain, sire!"

Frederick raised his forehead from the bed and looked sideways at her. Then for final glee, he hunched harder, once, twice, thrice, and his laughter was low and gurgling as Mary tried to climb from under the cruel punishment. But when he withdrew a bit, she tried to follow his prick, her giggles proving that she had understood the game. While he lay, waiting for his prick to cease throbbing, she fucked it with small, inept movements and to his surprise and delight, she seemed to have another cum.

"I perceive your cunt to be insatiable," he murmured.

"It is very good, sire," she panted. "I do not understand what occurs but I like it when the feeling comes so strong. Is it supposed to be part of my punishment, sire?"

Frederick chuckled. "Perhaps." He rolled away, his cock sliding out of her cunt with strings of curdled cum dragging across her thigh. It was only half relaxed; he felt as if he could fuck the inflamed and swollen little quim forever. It did small convulsions, sending his jism out on slow dribbling globes. He put his fingers there and smeared the sticky oozing over her pubic mound and down to her asshole. Again, he thrust his finger in and screwed it knuckle deep. Mary squirmed and giggled.

"It is strange," she husked. "I feel it right inside!"

Frederick's cock snapped to instant rigidity, the puffed foreskin folding back so the conical head of his organ seemed even larger than it was. He had been pleasantly surprised that the twelve-year-old girl had taken so much of his prick in her vagina and now he worked his finger in her rectum with new and exciting intent.

"Would you like to be fucked there, Mary?" he asked.

She blinked. "I—I do not think so, sire! It seems so small as I look at your great huge thing!"

He tried it first by having her get to her hands and knees while he stood to the bed, his legs braced. Her asshole, soft and absorbing to his finger, would not even begin to open for his prick. She grunted and panted as he tried, turning and pushing and nearly ejaculating in the excitement of the intriguing frustration. Then he obtained a jar of his finest London pomade and coated his prick from tip to balls, and then fingered a generous daub into her rectum. This made his cock dimple deeply, until her flesh deformed in a huge funnel-shaped dimple, but entry past the severely strained anus was impossible.

"Oh sire, it feels so good just there—may we not try to do it further?" Mary pleaded, her body writhing in distress though she made no effort to evade him.

"It must go, it must go," he muttered, and while his prick ached from bending and straining, he plunged three fingers into her rectum and made her groan with the fury of his stretching. Again he tried but her anus now was swollen and tender and it seemed to resist even more completely the full breadth of his glans. Mary was beginning to cry softly when he could stand it no longer. He gripped her hips and with his cock nudged slightly, gave a tremendous lunge. For a second, he thought it had done the trick, but Mary gave a short scream of agony and somehow, fell out of his grasp.

"Oh, no, no, sire!" she pleaded. "Oh, you have hurt me so. And I fear I am in dire need of the chamber pot!"

"All right, wench," he half snarled. "Maybe a good shit will teach that stubborn bum a thing or two. In here!"

As she got up from the bed, he took her arm and led her to bath chamber. The big porcelain pot with its lid sat in one corner. Frederick dragged it to the center of the small chamber, sloshing the lime water noisily.

"There," he said. "Get your reluctant ass onto it, Mary."

"I think I can m-manage, sire," she said, suddenly shy.

"Sit down and shit!" he snarled, and pressed her to a seat.

Her tears were quick, but as he stood above her, she began to evacuate with powerful eviction. Frederick stood, sweating and shaking and suddenly, he knew what to do. As Mary sighed in final relief, he jerked her off the pot and half-squatted, ramming his cock into her still oozing asshole. She shrieked, but he held her, excited by his ruthless victory. His prick was half buried in her rectum; he lifted her as he straightened up and carried her back to the bed. There, he let her brace herself, feet far apart and he held her hips and fucked into her distended bowel, paying no attention to her gasps and pleas for respite. And gradually, Mary arranged herself for his thrusting, her back bowed forward, her knees far apart. Every thrust seemed to peel the skin from his thundering organ, his cock ran in and out in long, ecstatic strokes, and his pleasure was so furious he could hardly breathe. Nor did she shirk the nearly twenty centimeters of prick he sent in with such fire. He reached under and felt of her cunt, wide open and pulsing as his cock pumped in her deep inner parts. He roughed her clitoris, making her tremble between sobs, and presently, she was not crying but mewling and panting to his fuck. He wasn't sure and did not care if she had cum or not, but when his came, a monstrous explosion of his balls that sent the jism spurting into her bowel with agonizing force, his knees gave way and his senses momentarily went blue-black. He let her fall, and like a man struck dumb, he saw how his cock slipped out of her ass and spat once or twice in final glee. Even then he stared at Mary's bottom, the two small cheeks spread wide and browned between. Her anus gaped, showing the wounded inner pink, crawling and convulsing in agony. Like a half-dead man, Frederick fell to the bed, laughing in gasping gutturals at the cruel victory of his indomitable prick.

six

For the size of his fist and the hardness of his knuckles, Jan's knock on Frederick's door was soft. He stood, ears attentive to the laughter of the fluffies in other rooms on the second story, his mind scheming to get a good bit closer to one or two of them once the matter of Marlene was settled to the master's satisfaction. He knocked again.

"Who is it?" came Frederick's question.

"Jan, sir."

"A moment!"

Jan waited. He could hear soft shufflings in the room, then the sound of the door bolts being released. A moment later, he was facing Frederick Tensington II, who seemed most disheveled and wore a worried look on his handsome face.

"Jan, yes, just the man I need! Come in!" He opened the door hardly wide enough to admit the grounds-keeper's huge body. Inside a step, Jan stared, but Frederick urged him on in and rebolted the heavy door.

Lying on the bed, her slim naked body as quiet as death, was Mary Fedren. Her legs were outthrust at a peculiar angle. In one glance around the room, Jan understood the scene. It was obvious that the master of Tensington had been vigorously fucking the child for some time. The bed was fouled and Mary's crotch was soiled and matted. Jan controlled his private anger over having lost his personal pussy to the half-stud he thought Frederick to be.

"Is she dead, sir?" he asked as Frederick sank to a weary seat in an elegant chair.

Frederick shook his head. "No. No. But her hips—she seems unable to stand or even get her legs to function!"

Jan walked over and looked down at the still form. Her eyes were half open, mere slits of silent agony. He looked at her cunt, swollen, lacerated and foul. Her belly and thighs were a mass of fine scratches, vivid testimony to a man's clutching lust. When Jan lifted one of the slender legs, Mary screamed shortly and panted like a wounded hare. He saw that her asshole was now as swelled and puffed as milk goat in heat. Her buttocks were coated with smeared shit, as if Frederick had tried to wipe away the evidence of his bestiality. Familiar with many things, including the husbandry of the estate's stock, Jan felt of Mary's hips. He found the joint failure easily.

"One hip joint is out of socket, Master Tensington," he said. "As if she had been spread beyond the limitations of her ligaments."

A sob of anguish escaped Frederick's lips. "But I did not mean to—she seemed so eager, so willing for all I could do!"

"Aye, but it sometimes happens with the very young. I recall once in Lancashire—a wench astraddle my legs with my cod well into her bum hole, became so excited she sprung herself, sir." Jan chuckled. "Even then, she insisted I finish her fucking before she fainted! Young ones have excitements no longer present in their mothers."

Frederick leaped to his feet, seizing both of Jan's thick upper arms. "Then you must know what to do with her! I am greatly distressed by this, groundskeeper, and I will be grateful if you know of some solution! My guests have a most peculiarly acrid sense of humor and I would not care to have them aware of this child's weaknesses! You will do what needs to be done, Jan Macklin!"

"Yes, sir. I will try."

He slipped the coil of his whip from his shoulder and removed his jacket. It was her left hip joint, he was sure. Disregarding her moans of pain, he turned her to her right side, the sprung joint forcing her leg up and forward at an awkward angle. He gripped the ankle with his massive fist. Deliberately, he worked the leg in a small circle, causing Mary to wail and gasp as the vital pain tore into her already anguished body. Then with a cat-like speed, Jan brought his left fist down in a tremendous blow precisely where her thigh bone junctured with her hip. A dull sound, like the breaking of a wet stick followed the smack of fist on flesh. Mary only let out a half cry before the pain rendered her unconscious. But when Jan again waggled and rotated her leg, the joint moved freely. He dropped the ankle. Mary lay, fainted, although her body trembled from unconscious responses.

"It is done! You've put it back in place!" Frederick gasped.

"I've done it often with sheep," Jan confessed.

"Will she be all right, now, groundskeeper?"

Jan grinned and shrugged. "Perhaps. She may be stiff there, but being slightly crippled is not going to hamper one as cock hungry as this one is!"

"She—she was not a virgin," Frederick said with a defensive tone. He straightened his lace-bordered shirt and rubbed his trousers into sleek fitting along his hips. "Well, groundskeeper?"

"If you will excuse my forwardness, sir, I would suggest that the matter is not ended here."

"What?" Frederick asked in alarm. "What do you mean?"

Jan's cunning was joined by his instinctive cruelty. He saw that his employer was afraid, and none too steady as to nerves. "Even now, she is beginning to open her eyes. Within a short time, she will be telling one and all that the Master Tensington has bum-fucked and codded her the entire day and that her leg stiffness is due to his furious passion, it having disjointed her in a moment of thrusting into her backside. There is a mat-

ter of Joseph Fedren, her father, who is a freeman even
though he has spent his life at Tensington, as his father
and grandfather before him. His outraged voice has
good claim upon the magistrate's ear, sir. One works
the freeman and often cheats him of his due, but one
does not rape his daughter, front and rear!" Jan stood,
his heart thumping with inner glee as he watched Frederick's face turn from flush to death gray. He pressed
his brutal advantage. "Joseph may not return from
Watertown until Tuesday next, I having anticipated a
need for his extended absence from Tensington. But
on Monday, the child here, is due at school, sir, and if
she does not go, questions will be asked. If she does
hobble the three kilometers, all will want to know of
her adventures as chamber maid in the Tensington
manse."

Frederick's eyes narrowed. "You draw a most impressive picture, groundskeeper. One, I think, that needs
consideration!"

"Aye, sir. Nor do I forget that even now, this poor
torn child's mother acts as jailer to your previous in-
discretion, the beautiful and famous Miss Marlene de
la Sage. Tillie Fedren is not one to forgive or forget
this kind of thing—" Jan finished with a dramatic
sweep of his hand that went the length of Mary's stirring, quivering body.

Frederick turned away and again sank to a weary
seat. "You plague me, groundskeeper," he muttered. "I
refuse to be plagued! All that has happened seemed a
natural progression of circumstances. I have consciously
done no wrong, and thusly, will not permit such ill-born
people to harass my position or mental comfort! And I
do not appreciate your smugly superior attitude, Jan

Macklin! I pay you well and overlook your transgressions! I will hear your solutions to the problems you have remarked."

"I am a simple country man, sir, and have no solutions. But I think the girl, here, represents the greatest danger to yourself."

By then, Mary was trying to sit up, her face streaked with tears, her hands kneading the monstrous soreness of her hips. Frederick abruptly got up and went to her, kneeling, less in apology than in an effort to face her at her own level.

"Mary Fedren," he said. "What has happened has been unfortunate. I know of your distress and hope it ends forthwith! But more agony can occur unless you understand that what I did I did in adoration of your slim beauty. And you must recall that not once did you protest my actions! It now behooves you to act the lady you are, and consider the consequences of revealing to anyone, your mother, your father, or your school friends, the nature of your adventure with me. It must remain a secret among the three of us, must it not? And I will reward you handsomely for your closed mouth. Is it agreed?"

Mary blinked, then opened her mouth to speak. After a moment of struggle, she burst into fresh tears. "No, no! I want my mama! Oh, you have hurt me and I think I am going to d-die! Oh, Mama, Mama! I can not stand it any more!"

"Mary! Mary, listen to me. You may rest here in my apartments and I will see that you are attended. There will be fine food and cakes and some new clothes for you, and by tomorrow, the pain will be gone and you may go home as if nothing had ever occurred!"

She jerked her shoulder from Frederick's frantic grasp and fell back on the bed, weeping furiously. Frederick, realizing he was on his knees before a simple farmer's daughter, rose and shook himself back into control.

"I think, sir, that you have not spoken to her in the language a woman understands best!" Jan said. Then he reached to the table and took from it his whip. Silently, he held it out to Frederick.

Frederick's face changed several times in swift response. At first, his eyes opened in surprise, then they narrowed in speculation, and finally, he looked down at the weeping girl with the eyes of a hawk about to pounce on a hedgerow hare. He extended a trembling hand and took the whip, shaking it out on the expensive rug underfoot. Jan stepped back, knowing well that with the thick leather butt in his hand, Frederick had ceased to fear or worry, and that the innate cruelty of the Tensingtons was singing in the young man's blood. His acute perception also noticed that in the few seconds he had held the whip, his cock had become a prominent ridge in his London trousers. Jan stepped back.

Suddenly, Frederick lashed out and down, the inexpert stroke laying the whip the length of Mary's body without a popping finish. She shrieked, turning to face this new torment just as Frederick lashed again. The line of red ran from Mary's shoulder to her thigh and she clutched herself, screaming. Frederick laid a cut across her arms and back again. He was panting heavily, his face a mask of insane excitement. He struck again, finally managing to make the lash tips bite. Several drops of blood welled from the wound on Mary's shoulder.

"Now, you dirty little slut!" Frederick raged. "Tell me that you will do as I demand or I will flay your skin from your fucking body! Tell me!" He cut at her again before she could answer.

She screamed and twisted, falling to her face. "Oh, no, no! I will never tell, never. I promise never to t-tell! I do!"

But it was too late, Jan could see. Frederick, fired by his sadistic burst, excited by her small bottom, as yet untouched by the lash, began to lay the whip in ripping blows across her body. An unholy grin cleft his face, his eyes seemed ready to burst from his skull. The louder Mary cried out, the harder his blows became. She huddled, trying to cover herself with inadequate arms and he took fierce delight in striking every exposed place on her ribboned skin he could find.

Nor could Jan interfere. He stood back, watching the brutal play, his own sensuality rising in leaps. The tortured little body had lost its identity to Jan, as had the man who lashed so frenziedly. His cock was rising with monstrous swelling, his balls throbbed with urgency. Mary's screams and the whistle and pop of the whip were a symphony to his ears and it all seemed blended in the spray of blood.

Abruptly, Frederick seemed to freeze, as if his mind had snapped. He dropped the whip, his fingers worked spastically. Then he tore at his trousers and as his cock leaped free, he leaped upon Mary's back, shagging like a dog after an overheated bitch. Her howl of agony was only one more inspiration to Frederick. His ass came high as his trousers dropped away and he grunted down to whatever hole he had entered.

Then Jan's control snapped. He snatched up the whip and laid one fierce, snapping blow across Frederick's exposed buttocks. Now Jan stood, ripping open his own trousers as he stared into Frederick's bare ass, devouring the hairy rounds with the sack of balls below, barely shrouding the manner in which Frederick's cock plowed into Mary's reraped bum hole. With his own prick in hand, Jan moved and fell forward. Frederick's scream mingled with Mary's, but as his prick found entry, Jan humped up and forced it into the asshole of his frenzied master. His big arms came down and around the bodies under him and he tied the three of them together in irrevocable piling. Only when his buried prick sent contented messages to his brain did Jan realize what he had done. He started to rear away and was surprised that Frederick's ass raised in following. Raised enough for Mary to scramble from under and Jan let her go. His hands closed under Frederick's body and one found the long, pole-hard prick, still slippery from its coursing in Mary's asshole. He fucked in hard, and the gust of air from Frederick's lungs was not in distress. He came to his hands and knees, bracing against the deep, long-stroking Jan. Jan rearranged his own knees, fitting them together in close meshing. He lay hard to Frederick's back, his under hand stroking the throbbing prick with firm fascination. Somewhere to the back or side, Mary's sobbing came in choked irregularity. Jan plumbed the delectable bowel of Frederick and let his balls knock to more balls. In the milking anus, his prick seemed twice its normal hugeness and excitement. In his mind, the image of

Mary, lying under the cutting whip loomed until all other thoughts were crowded out. As his cum approached, Jan gripped Frederick's cock in a death-tight hand. Frederick screamed and twisted as Jan jerked and half-crushed the organ. Ramming deep, Jan held, his jism bursting free in ecstatic spewing. His hand released Frederick's cock and in a split second, the wounded pole began to pump cum out onto the bed. Both men writhed together, their passions blanking all thought of what they did, one in the other.

Jan recovered first. He seemed stunned for a moment, then he reared from Frederick's sagging body and dragged his immense cock from the inflamed bum. He had also lost his trousers, they hung about his knees and he stood in a holding arch, his prick dripping, its color changed to mal-odorous brown. He looked around and Mary was huddled in a corner, her eyes wide, her body half crouched. He grinned at her, and she bit her lip a moment before smiling back.

"Groundskeeper, I'll have you hanged!" Frederick roared, then he laughed. "Fucked in the ass by a renegade Scot and damme if I didn't like it! Where is that little slut? Ah, there you are, you darling! Come to me and let me kiss your tears away!"

"Yes, oh, yes, sire!" she panted and hobbled to his outstretched hands. "Oh, you were so beautiful as he fucked you! And I don't hurt too much from the whip, sire, I really don't! Oh, Jan, my leg is f-fine, now!"

Jan laughed uproariously. "Tillie, my lovely one, you had a good one when your ass opened up for her!" Then he waddled off to the bath chamber to wash his limping cod.

Tea was a long affair because there was more brandy than tea. Frederick stood in the arched doorway to the music room, his freshly scrubbed face a mask of mixed emotions. His asshole throbbed and his prick ached, but he wished these lascivious guests were on their way back to London; his mind was busy with the new excitements he had discovered amid his own personal surroundings. But there was a precaution or two to take, because Marlene de la Sage had been absent since early morning. It was now dusk and before long, one of her friends might well be curious about her prolonged non-appearance.

They were a lethargic group now, fucked out, sucked out and lying about in a state of careless sensualism. Frederick could hardly remember their names. The women, having forsaken their stylish coiffures and the voluminous under-garments of the times, lolled, with legs spraddled to ease the chafing and breasts half exposed as they drank and made low throaty laughter and words with the London gentry. Here and there a slowly moving hand was buried in the folds of a half-drawn skirt, and Malcomb Fageol, really the driving force in these affairs, was leaning heavily over a slender blonde girl whose name seemed to be Hazel, in Frederick's mind. Hazel, Anne, Matilda, Joyce and a plump vixen named Sherry, all bursting with sexual urgency, all indifferent to time, the cock or the un-English intimacy of a whore-fest.

Because Malcolm had secured the presence of the innocent Marlene in this group, Frederick went first to him, ignoring the ribald comments of the women about

"—damned long time tidying up with that little split-tail!" and "—show us the teeth marks, Freddie!"

"Something, Freddie?" Malcolm asked, his eyes less frivolous than his tone of voice.

"Perhaps, but not really. I thought I ought to tell you all that Miss Marlene deserted our little party shortly after lunch. I hadn't noticed that she was gone until my stable man informed me that she had asked for a carriage to return to London. My fault, I suppose. I had a bit to drink last night and wasn't the best of hosts!"

Malcomb sat up, a furrow on his brow. "Back to London? Oh, come on! That isn't like Marlene! She's generally the gayest one at a party. Any reason?"

"The stable man said she kept remarking an important engagement she had forgotten. At any rate, her bags are gone and so is she! I do hope you'll tender my apologies to the lady when you return to London, Malcomb, old chap."

"Yes. Yes. Were you a problem to her, last evening, Freddie?"

One of the girls laughed. "I'd say he could be a problem or he could be no problem at all! Depends on how he approached her!"

Frederick carried it off with easy quips and ribald replies. But he wasn't sure Malcomb Fageol believed the lie, or if he did, had some worry about what the actress might remark among her London friends. Or perhaps, what the London friends might tell her about Malcomb Fageol, the most active, unpaid procurer in the upper-middle class circles of the theater. Frederick didn't much care how Malcomb thought; the lie was told, the actress's absence explained, at least momentarily. There was still the problem of his actual disposition of Marlene, but the magnificent manner of controlling Mary had given him confidence in Jan's ability to arrange a peaceful good-bye to Marlene. He drank some, talked some and relaxed. In a separate chamber, Mary lay tucked in bed, a dram of laudanum soothing her remaining pains, and a promise of fine treatment stilling her childish mind.

If his thoughts were scattered, so were his emotions and he realized this when he found himself making positive efforts to evade and discourage the sole-eyed brunette named Joyce. Her perfume annoyed him, her idle words and surreptitious thigh pressures left him indifferent. Finally, on pretense of checking the progress of their later dinner, he left the group and made his way to his father's old study. There he sat, slouched in the big leather chair and contemplated himself and the erotic events of the afternoon.

It had begun, not with the entry of Jan Macklin, but an hour or so prior to that. He had been so enamoured of Mary's slim young body and her apparent delight in being fucked, no matter how, that he had lost track of time and probability. How Jan had known he had been fucking madly in Mary's bum when her hip joint popped out, Frederick did not know, but Jan had been correct. At first, he had thought her screams were just more joy, more excitement and more ecstasy. Not until he had dragged his prick from her asshole and stared down at her writhing body had he decided something was wrong.

A long hour or two had passed then, while she lay groaning and crying on the bed, her legs out-pushed, her belly heaving. He had not known what to do, but he had been monstrously fascinated and excited by what he had done. Hard-fucked as he had been, he had still stood over her agonized body and masturbated onto her squirming form. Then had come the concern, and subsequently, Jan Macklin.

He thought about Jan. Employee that he was, he yet had the strange ability to make one feel his power and his superiority. He pretended subservience even while he wrested authority from his betters and tortured them with his calm while they were excited. How surely, Frederick thought, had Jan handed him the whip and told him what to do about the reluctant Mary. The rest was wispy in Frederick's mind. Beating the already suffering girl had been one of the most exciting and pleasurable times of his life, only slightly less pleasant than the humiliating attack on his bum and cock the unfearing Jan had made in the delightful moments when he was further punishing Mary with his thundering prick. It did not bother Frederick that he had submitted to, and enjoyed, a faggot's delight as Jan's gigantic cock had plowed and distended his bum hole. He was not concerned that in not securing a pistol and shooting Jan, he had forever placed the man in a position to demand and command. His one worry was that he could not again seek these mysterious thrills without asking the groundskeeper for assistance. The single item Frederick feared was the cold look of disdain Jan turned upon him and the tone of the boisterous laughter the man produced at other people's discomforts.

He also thought it a travesty of his position that a country lout and a small child seemed to know and understand so much about sensual delights. Frederick forced himself to be patient. In a few days, Mary's body would rebound with the pliability of youth. The guests would be gone and Marlene would be somehow placated. Then he would call Jan Macklin and together, they would plan and execute another of the exciting sessions. He, himself, would need a day or so because his asshole felt as raw as if he had been shitting bramble points.

———————

Even in the deepening dusk, his aim was perfect. Jan stood in a lazy slouch and picked this leaf or that from a bush, his senses enjoying the pop of the lash as he imagined the whip kissing the tender hide of a helpless woman. Or Frederick Tensington's hairy ass. He grinned. At the time it had seemed a delightful asshole, but he hadn't cared much for the shit-smeared rump when the passion had passed. Jan was a man who liked soft, white flesh, resilient and alive with nerves he could hurt. He liked hair, growing on a woman's quim, in her armpits and if she were the meaty sort, up the crack of her ass where it seemed to add impact to her sensuality. He loved a protesting bum hole, but Frederick's hadn't protested. There was also the abomination of the eternal cock and the sagging balls. He had masturbated Frederick, but his intention in jerking and twisting the excited prick had been to hurt the man, not give him violent orgasm. Jan moved slowly, his nightly guard less than interesting.

Once, he thought of strolling down to the Fedren cottage.

He had a second thought because he was not quite sure how Frederick intended to deal with the questionable situation of Miss Marlene. Once returned to London among her friends—and her private physician, she was capable of stirring up a chamber pot of stink. While none of the basic guilt was his, Jan knew the way of gentry. They would turn to him if Frederick's desperation caused a raised finger of accusation, and in any magistrate's court, the master's word was many times as weighty as the groundskeeper's.

Not being a man of panic, Jan controlled his concerns. She was only a frantic cunt.

seven

She had slept because there was little else she could do. Now Marlene lay with slitted eyes, watching Tillie Fedren mend some of her daughter's drab dresses. Her face was stolid, her strong hands steady, not at all the tender, caressive things Marlene remembered them to be.

She shuddered with revulsion, not alone for the raw passion Tillie had created, but for her own responses. For two days, she had been buffeted with unbelievable emotions and her body had suffered every conceivable indignity, and underlying it all was the blanket of panic no amount of logic could dispel. Like now. She was being held in physical bondage for some reason beyond her imagination, and beyond Tillie's ability to explain. Escape seemed impossible; once during a brief trip to the rear outhouse, she had stumbled deliberately to test Tillie's alertness. The alertness was instantly proved, as was the strength of Tillie' arms and hands.

But there had been some softening of Tillie's attitude since their moments of passion together. She untied Marlene's hands when it was time to eat and she had furnished a rather worn and ragged hairbrush so Marlene could straighten her tangled locks. The fact that Tillie had insisted on retying Marlene after this interlude had been partially explained by her recitation of the many cruelties Jan Macklin was capable of. Marlene thought that if this nightmare continued very much longer and she showed some warmth to the peculiar intensity of Tillie's sensuality, more softening might produce a chance for escape, or for headlong flight that might end in merciful death. She stirred.

"Tillie?"

The woman put down her sewing and peered through the developing dusk in the sparsely windowed cottage. "Yes?"

"Could I have some tea—something hot? My hands and feet are so cold! Lack of circulation, I suppose. Please, Tillie?"

Tillie stood up, smiling slightly. She had neglected to rebutton her bodice, deliberately or by chance, and the swell of her full tits formed an intriguing valley in her suntanned flesh. She moved to the stone fireplace and stirred the coals before she swung the iron pot around and over the smoldering fire. Then she came to the bed and sat close, her hip against Marlene's. One hand dropped and petted the flared shape under the coverlet. A tinge of fright went through Marlene as she saw the slight flare of Tillie's nostrils, but at the same instant, her cunt did a small twitching. She turned her head away from the steady gaze Tillie sent down to her.

"No, no more, Tillie!" Marlene breathed. "I can't stand your fingers and lips again! I'm so afraid, so stricken with panic! Whatever is going to happen to me? Oh, what else have they in store?"

"Now then, don't you fret, Marlene," Tillie murmured, her hand still smoothing its way over Marlene's belly. "We'll have tea presently and you'll feel better. Then we'll talk some more."

"I—I don't want to talk," Marlene breathed. "What is there to talk about?"

"Nice things," Tillie replied in a firmer tone. She got up and made the tea. When it was steaming in cracked cups on the crude stand beside the bed, she leaned over Marlene and began to untie her wrists. The weight of her big tits hung low, once brushing Marlene's cheek, and the warm odor of woman, not too well washed, pressed down in overwhelming force. Marlene whimpered, feeling herself quiver in memory. When both wrists were freed, Tillie helped her sit up, the blanket falling around Marlene's waist to expose her own bulbous tits. In rubbing her wrists, she set the twin globes to rolling and bouncing and when Tillie's hands went to them in gentle adoration, Marlene's eyes closed in anticipated horror.

"Feel of me," Tillie breathed, shaking her tits free of her dress. "Oh, Marlene, we are here together, both captives of Jan Macklin in our different ways! I have a little and you have nothing! Must we fight the single blessing each of us has in each other? Oh, you are so beautiful, so vital, so compelling to me!"

Abruptly stricken with pity for the whimpering woman, Marlene put a palm to Tillie's cheek, then let it slip down her strong neck to the exciting firmness of her bare tit. Her fingers trembled; she had never touched another woman's breast before and the resilient flesh, vibrating with lift and eagerness was fiery hot. She touch the nipple, feeling its subtle throb as it hardened swiftly. Then as if in mutual understanding, she and Tillie were tit to tit in a furious embrace.

"You see, my dear, there are lots of things to talk about," Tillie whispered in her ear. "Delightful things! Have your tea!"

Shaking with confusion, Marlene sipped slowly at her tea. With equal slowness, breathing very hard, Tillie laid back the coverlet, baring Marlene's naked belly and out-veed legs, tied in a wide spreading to the foot of the old bed. Marlene looked down at her crotch, wondering if the throb of her cunt were visible. It lay deep in the auburn curls, the swollen lips slightly apart so the enlivened pink of her inner tissues peeked out sweetly. Sight of her own sex was as disturbing as Tillie's hands, kneading and massaging her tired thighs on the slow journey to the important juncture of body and legs. Abruptly, Tillie stood up and went to the cottage door. She opened it a bit and peered out, this way and that, then she closed and bolted it.

Standing at the foot of the bed, Tillie began unbuttoning the rest of her dress, and as Marlene stared, the woman divested herself of the drab garment and stood naked in a proud arch. Marlene gasped. Tillie was less than classical at hip and bust and there were a few fine blue veins on her white thighs. But she was voluptuously meaty, entrancingly full-fleshed and very much alive. Her belly showed a slight outcurve over the bushy vee at her crotch, and as Marlene inventoried the sensual body, Tillie's hands traveled from her inner thighs, up, smoothing out and then over the smooth torso to the ponderous bulbs of her tits.

"I am not as pretty as you, Marlene," she murmured. "If I am beautiful it is inside where my blood races and my nerves scream for your touch! Oh, we must be naked together!

A moment of alien excitement came to Marlene as Tillie untied her ankles, bending and twisting with impatient haste. But it was useless and Marlene knew it; the woman was too strong and the door was bolted and outside, the dusk was rapidly becoming darkness. Further, she was in a lonely cottage, hidden somewhere in the semi-woods, her sense of direction was askew and she could as well run headlong into Jan Macklin or the evil Tensington as she could escape to some neighboring village. And there was another drug in her veins, the insidious stirring as she looked at Tillie, the tingle of her skin like a subtle itch as she absorbed the sensual impact of the moment.

In relief, she drew up each leg as it was freed, her hips protesting, her feet tingling as the blood moved past the circle of red where the ropes had been.

"No, Marlene, I will do it for you!" Tillie husked. She crawled onto the bed and knelt so that when she lifted Marlene's left leg, placing it on her shoulder, then the right, she was positioned not unlike a man about to mount the surrendered body below. She began then, to massage each leg from thigh to ankle, all the while burning Marlene's crotch with fire-hot eyes. In turn, Marlene stared into Tillie's crotch, surprised by the neat plump rolls of dark flesh, made increasingly mysterious by the enveloping darkness.

"It is so dark—we need a lamp," someone said and Marlene was surprised to find it was her own voice, pleading for illumination of the splendid body in front of her.

"Yes, a lamp!" Tillie exclaimed. Reluctantly, she climbed from the bed and with a broomstraw, carried a light from the fire to the dangling overhead lamp. To fire the wick, she stood on her toes and the resultant stretch was magnificent as the kerosene ignited and cast soft, flickering highlights down the mass of jiggling curves. Smiling, Tillie came back to the bed but she did not resume her massage. She lay out beside Marlene and they closed in embrace, hands fluttering in lewd release as their lips met in a furious mashing. Marlene, who had never put her hands to a naked body other than her own, was so excited by the feel of soft, writhing shapes she could hardly breathe. Turning hard to Tillie, she threw one leg over the firm hip and nearly screamed into her mouth as her own cunt pressed firmly to Tillie's thigh. Together, they rocked, each moving to facilitate some pressure or to simply thrill at the sensations of skin rubbing to skin.

Marlene could think of nothing; her hands filled with flesh, a deformed tit against her own, a straining strip of back muscle, a taut full nate, beside another as taut. Her own body rejoiced at each pressure of Tillie's fingers, her mouth ached with the wet fury of their kissing.

Gradually, they slowed their frenzy, contenting their rising emotions with more subtle feelings. As a moment of stunned delight occurred to her, Marlene released the delicious body and Tillie turned, reversing their positions. The lamp flickered, and the dancing lights around Tillie's spraddled ass, now poised above Marlene's face, made the curves and hollows and sensual shapes as beautiful as dawn over rolling hills. Marlene stared into the deep valley that faded down to the hairy rolls, now parted to show the lobed inner mouth of Tillie's cunt. And when Tillie's lips mashed hard to her quim, sending a shudder of ecstasy through Marlene, she knew what to do. Raising her head, she planted an open lipped kiss to Tillie's sex. Her gasp was a sputter into the moist, hot nest. Her tongue darted out, returned in quivering at the sudden acrid taste, turning sweet as she worked her throat in constricted surprise. Then Tillie let her ass settle and Marlene thrust her face into the exquisite fire, her lips and tongue fighting awkwardly for the right thing to do. Her hips seemed to know. As Tillie's tongue began a rhythmic licking, Marlene discovered the up-hunching and twisting to match the caress. A second or so later, Tillie taught her another marvel; Marlene moaned as the finger burrowed and screwed into her anus, sending shrieks of different ecstasy through her already ecstatic body. She felt over Tillie's buttock, finding the soft pucker, thrilling at its rubbery invitation to the tip of her half-shy digit. Then she found Tillie's clitoris, a throbbing ridge, and her finger went into the delighted asshole with no hesitation. The feel was good, the wet inner tissues seemed to cling and beg and Marlene urged her finger in and in until she wept for additional joints to bury in the hot sleeve. In her own bum, the finger was coursing and like an obedient child, she assumed the plunging in Tillie's ass. They lay, less violent now but deeply engrossed in the pleasures of their tandem fuck, their mutual suck, both floating on some impossible sea of excruciating joy.

Because orgasm was still a strange and wonderful ultimate to Marlene, she had hers with no warning. It came as a rolling wave of strength and weakness, thudding in her brain in tempo to the convulsions in her cunt. She screeched into Tillie's vagina, her mouth abruptly a hard shell of probing, her tongue caught in the oozing depths. She felt Tillie change her buttock action, felt the furious down pressure of the open, saliva dripping cunt, and she guessed the sweet moment had come to her squirming, panting partner. Then Marlene relaxed, whimpering into the weight of a sex as weary as her own.

Malcomb Fageol had not even suspected there was a cottage in the dark-shrouded woods until the lamp came on, a slow glow at first which developed into a dancing yellow square, divided into six small panels and edged by half-looped curtains. Slowly, feeling his way along the unfamiliar path, he approached the small house. A poor one, he was sure, hidden away in the wooded gully as if ashamed of its inadequacy. He made no effort to weight probabilities. He was looking for Marlene de la Sage, whom he had never believed had returned to London.

A dozen reasons supported his doubts of the casual story Frederick Tensington had told. For one, Marlene was not an adventurous girl, nor a stupid one. Frederick was a frantic stud, a man given to wild flights of sexual fancy and with cock in hand, he had many times ceased to be a gentleman. Malcomb had, as usual, brought Frederick a virgin beauty, leaving it to Frederick to work his way into her quim in a maner calculated against victory, not defeat. It was accepted knowledge that Frederick had spent most of the night in Marlene's bedchamber. But subtle inquiry had discovered for Malcomb that no one recalled having seen Marlene since she had excused herself the previous evening and disappeared on Frederick's arm.

The doubt lay heaviest when he remembered Marlene. She was an articulate girl and one possessed of rightful courage, both as a natural heritage and a success that bred confidence in a woman. If she had remembered an engagement in London, she would have come to them all—especially himself—and made her excuses for departure.

If she had suffered a few of Frederick's invariable tricks, ranging from his often stated desire to beat a woman into mad passions, or to choke her half to death with his cock, or to surprise her as she lay in gentle afterglow with a hard length of prick up her unsuspecting ass, then Marlene's return to London was not hard to justify—except that she would have publicly castigated the errant Frederick, dramatic castigations being one of her strong roles on the state.

So now he stood, mid-way in his search for Marlene de la Sage. With no reason to believe she was outside the manse, he had made a round of the immediate grounds, speaking quietly to those he saw, trying to find some indication of where the young beauty might be. Not in this mean cottage, he was sure, but because he was a man of many sensualities, he moved to the lighted window in hopes of perhaps catching some country lass in dishabille.

Two country lasses and not in dishabille. Malcomb found himself staring into two of the most delicious asses, bare as babes, he had seen in some time. The two women lay in tight embrace, feeling, kissing and rolling together in complete abandon. The light was not good enough for him to see facial details, but the dancing shadows created by their undulating hips and flailing legs entranced him sufficiently he did not care what they looked like. Sweat broke out on Malcomb's brow as he watched the lewd play of crotch on crotch. He had seen many lascivious exhibitions, in bawdy houses and private rooms; the raging drama on the old old bed in the poor cottage was a hundred times more impressive, aided by the fact that he was a silent, secret witness to the lesbian affair.

When they suddenly switched ends, he still did not know the face the Rubenesque woman plunged into the broadly spread crotch. Her hair was unfashionable and she was obviously of the country. That she knew how to suck a willing cunt, even to the deliberate insertion of a finger in the delectable asshole of the underwoman, was obvious to Malcomb. He squirmed as the bobbing head was met by the hunching cunt and it was equally apparent that the mouth to pussy act was being duplicated at the other end of the squirming pile. Not one whit abashed, Malcomb opened his trousers and took out his swelling prick. Finding a firmer stance at the window, he stared in massive appreciation as he slowly stroked his cock to ease its pulsating demand.

But he did not let his prick respond when the frenzied thrashing on the bed turned into cum antics. There was more, he was sure. The woman whose head was to the window, raised and patted the spread ass into which she had just been kissing. Her fingers opened and probed the pulsing cunt, lovingly and with some talent. Then she turned and came to a seat beside the other woman, who instantly rose to a hard embrace.

Malcomb's mouth opened to shout, but he did not. His cock went half soft in his fist at the shock of seeing Marlene de la Sage in lesbian embrace with the handsome if unbeautiful woman who was obviously a farmer's wife. The why of it seemed no mystery. He cursed his own naivete. All his London friends had said she was a virgin, unsusceptible to the best approaches they could make. Why not a virgin in their eyes, he mused. She was a lesbian, not like the boisterous and vulgar Anne Grange, but in a deeper, private way that had never leaked even a rumor of perversion to her professional friends.

And maybe, Frederick had been sincere, reporting what Marlene had no doubt paid a stable man to say; who would think to look for her in the arms of a lusty country woman if all thought the actress had returned to London? Malcomb relaxed his worry and regained the stiffness of his prick as the two women began to laugh and talk together while they fingered each other's considerable charms. He had been correct—there was going to be more.

The country bitch went to a corner of the meanly furnished cottage and returned with a thick-handled straw broom. Standing in front of Marlene, the woman went into a beautifully lewd crouch, and as she talked, applied the fat branch-handle to her quim. She urged it in, wincing and shivering, then laughing with Marlene as the latter put a hand to the broom and assisted its entry. Malcomb's breath choked in his throat as he watched the handle go in until it seemed certain to rest against the woman's stomach. He guessed at more than twenty centimeters, then with small wits left, observed the lewd glee with which the elegant darling of the theatrical world fucked her friend with the imposing stick. Few things he had ever witnessed shocked his equilibrium like the sight of the buxom woman going through the full ecstasies of cum in the standing position, her buttocks jumping, her tits swaying and bouncing in the throes of her lascivious passion. With the broom handle still buried in her cunt, she drew Marlene up and they embraced in eager frenzy. And there was going to be more, he told his thundering prick.

Marlene had turned to her hands and knees on the bed and the country woman, still trembling slipped the handle from her quim and applied it up into Marlene's spraddled rump. He thought at first it was in her bum hole, but as she began to roll and hump, he saw that she was being as avidly fucked as she had in turn screwed the other pussy, if not so unreasonably deep. Once the handle was in coursing, the country woman straddled the remaining handle, pulling it snugly up until it lay in the gash of her cunt, held by the powerful thighs in meaningful squeezing. The woman then put both hands to Marlene's waist and fucked her with the awkward movements of a lusty youth. It was not gentle. Marlene's head rolled from side to side then nodded high and low as the handle bumped deep into her vaginal canal. Her tits hung, swaying and snapping and her back rose and fell in ecstatic humping. When her cum came, she reared, then fell forward on her belly, gasping and writhing. The other woman took firm grip on the broomstick, front and rear and continued to masturbate her quim for several intense moments. Malcomb jerked at his prick and let it spew out to the wall of the cottage. But he had been impatient, he quickly saw, because there was going to be still more.

That it was going to be of a different nature he did not realize until Marlene rose up in obvious protest. The country woman kissed the actress, but her hands seemed strong and directive. To Malcomb's surprise, Marlene collapsed on her back, weeping profusely. She made no resistance as the woman tied her to the bed, wrists and ankles. He blinked. The ropes had been there all along; he had been so entranced by the writhing, passionate performance he had not seen the srtong ropes. He stared, not able to fully understand what he saw. Marlene, patently in the throes of anguish, strained and twisted against the firm bonds that held her in total spreading. The country woman stood, talking, but with evident sorrow. Through the thick stone walls came small high cries from Marlene. Her head raised, her face was drawn in fury as she berated the woman so recently her lover.

He was stunned then, when the woman leaned and swung her right palm with great force. He faintly heard the smack; Marlene stiffened and fell back, her belly heaving in positive distress. She struggled only a bit more before resigning herself to whatever fate the woman had decreed. Her own chest heaving in stress, the woman picked up the broom. For a moment, she contemplated it with bland features, then placed it to her lips and licked tentatively at the gleaming wet so recently churned from Marlene's quim. What she then did sent Malcomb's cock up in jerking stiffness.

Kneeling on the bed, she pressed Marlene's belly with one strong hand while the other fed the broom handle into the squirming crotch, too low, even if Malcomb hadn't been in a position to see, to penetrate the limpid cunt. Marlene's instant humping and twisting showed him how the blunt handle was a few centimeters into her bum hole. She tried to roll from side to side, her muscles straining as she reached the end of her tethers. The country woman continued to press the handle deeper, her own muscles standing out as she forced the brutal impalement past Marlene's instinctive resistance. When Marlene suddenly quieted, he thought he understood; the broom handle was now so deeply implanted every move she made was agonizing. The country woman worked the handle several times, each thrust seeming less obstructed than the previous one. Marlene now was merely shuddering, her tits shaking in response to the massive straining. Her eyes were closed, her mouth was agape, her tongue fluttering in an emotion more violent than passion.

The woman stood up, leaving the thick handle imbedded in Marlene's asshole. Malcomb could hardly believe the difference in the scene. The woman seemed angry, almost viciously so. Marlene, so recently an adoring devotee of their lewd play, was writhing in pain. The wrist and ankle ropes took on new significance to Malcomb. He searched the interior of the cottage with critical eyes; there was no sign of Marlene's London apparel, nor a single case or bag to witness her voluntary presence on her bed of torture. And the woman, dressing now, seemed calm and formidable, and strangely aloof from Marlene.

Occasionally, Marlene's hips twitched, causing the broom handle to move slightly, which in turn, made Marlene's mouth form shapes of anguish.

Her plight, plus the strange manner of her morning disappearance, added to his knowledge of Frederick Tensington's weird sexual tastes, gave Malcomb Fageol a sudden trembling. His prick went soft in his fist, and he hastily returned it to his trousers. He stared at the country woman, now sipping tea from a large mug. Her expression was unreadable. But abruptly, she put down the mug and went to the bed. With a swift jerk, she ripped the broom handle from Marlene's bum, reversed the utensil and stabbed straight into Marlene's exposed cunt with the stiff, hard straw. Once, twice, three times she stabbed, and when Marlene was stricken with a new fit of agony, the woman laughed and hurled the broom to a corner.

By then, Malcomb was very sure that Marlene de la Sage was a prisoner, despite her seeming willingness to join the woman in bold lesbian orgy. It would not be the first time a harassed woman had pretended to be a willing partner in obscenities to escape physical destruction.

Mumbling, weaving, his senses only half clear, Malcomb turned and hurried back to the manse. He had one or two very difficult decisions to make. Frederick Tensington might be innocent or guilty of conspiracy to destroy Marlene; in either case, all of Malcomb's well-being depended upon his unshakable reputation for discretion among the gentry. On the other hand, if London ever decided he was even partly to blame for the destruction and degradation of Marlene de la Sage, he could reserve a dungeon in Old Bailey for a long, long time. He leaned heavily toward no contact with Scotland Yard.

eight

"This is what I have seen," Malcomb finished, his hushed voice a loud thing amid the total silence from the group of shocked men. In the telling, it had lost its sensual impact and had become a brutal tale of ruthless perversion. "I do not know who the woman was, nor how Marlene came to be there. I only know that unless something is immediately done, London's darling is in grave danger of great physical harm, and perhaps a mental hysteria she can never overcome!"

"What have you decided, Malcomb?" Harvey Sanborne asked.

"Nothing, or I should have put the decision in action!

But, frankly, I hesitate to speak to our good host about it. He may—"

"But you must!" Alfred Stuntz broke in. "None of us are puritans nor desire to interfere, but the consequences of what you recount can be a worse plague than the Marseille clap! You must tell Frederick. He has men and authority. We must go immediately to her rescue. And if not a rescue, at least drag her from the charms of this country lesbian, even at the risk of disturbing some private desires. It can well be, you know, that Marlene inspired this entire affair without realizing it could get so far out of hand. We must find Frederick and see to the end . . . this abomination!"

"You suspect Frederick of some conspiratorial knowledge of all this? Even so, Marlene deserves our interference! We must act!"

Malcomb was still not certain their true obligation was not to go directly to the cottage and rescue Marlene. But with his friends' insistence about informing Frederick in a general hue and cry, he led them to Frederick's private chambers. Shortly after his first knock, the master of Tensington appeared, somewhat sleepy-eyed.

"What is wrong, my friends?" he asked, coughing shortly.

"We have discovered that Marlene did not go back to London!"

"She is here! The prisoner of a foul woman of the sod!"

"We need your help, Frederick! Send for your groundskeeper!"

Finally, Malcomb held up his hand for silence. With measured regard for what he thought to be the truth, he told Frederick what he had seen, omitting some of the delectable details which made his recounting even more gruesome than before. Frederick seemed aghast, and after re-establishing some of the details, he went roaring down the hall, calling for Jan Macklin. Servants scurried, and by the time they were in the main hall below, the burly figure of the groundskeeper came from the rear of the house, his shotgun clutched in one fist, his coiled whip in the other.

Brutally, Frederick retold the story. "Do you know the woman, my man?" he demanded.

"Yes sir. She is the wife of one of our field hands. Are you sure, sir, that the house is that by the creek?"

"I am sure," Malcomb spoke up. "Miss Marlene is there, a prisoner, suffering the foulest degradations it is possible to imagine. And we are wasting time, Frederick! We must go now!"

Malcomb saw the master of Tensington hesitate before he spoke: "Get a lantern and lead the way, Jan. I think we may not need your bird gun but will certainly need your whip. Do you understand?"

"Yes sir! One of the terrace lanterns will do," he said, leaning his shotgun against the wall. "We will see to this woman!"

For an instant, Malcomb had the distinct feeling that he had somehow loosed worse violence and evil than he had attempted to cure.

"There," the London fop said, pointing to the light.

"Aye, sir," Jan replied, as he didn't know exactly where the Fedren cottage lay. He moved on, the whip in his hand a comforting weight. He had never killed a human with it, but he knew he was going to presently; he had read the desperation and the determination in Frederick's eye and for his own part in the affair, Jan preferred a dead Tillie to a live and voluble one. He winced inwardly over a private loss. She was the best fuck on the Tensington estate, and he was going to kill her with his whip. Her daughter was a fair bid for second fucking honors and she was now a confirmed protege of the lusty Frederick. At the entrance to the cottage gate, he stopped and looked back at his entourage. Frederick was closest, then the fop who had uncovered the mess with his snooping. Behind them, there were several men and a few of the fluffies. Jan held up his hand.

"Remain here," he whispered harshly. "I will break in the door, if necessary, and secure the woman. You may then come after."

"Good man," Frederick muttered. "Go, then!"

At the door, Jan hesitated. It was quiet behind the plank barrier. He knew the size and strength of the hickory bolt and it would, by his orders, be in secure place. The bed was to the right, and there was some room in which to swing. Tillie would be in her favorite rocker, or perchance, with the actress at the bed. In either case, there was nowhere for her to run, nor to evade him. He also knew the easy way would be to knock and call, then step back and meet her with the whip when she opened the door. This he thought, might make the London gentry suspicious. He drew a breath preparatory to sending his fifteen stone against the door. He lunged.

The hickory bar held but the wrought iron hinges parted with a crash that filled the night. Jan stopped, saw Tillie as she leaped to her feet, mouth open in shock and fear. His whip flicked out, and he cut one corner of her mouth open a full two inches, instantly ending any chance of her saying a word. She screamed, a bloody gurgling wail and he cut the other corner open so her jaw dropped in a flood of gushing blood. She stumbled back, clutching her face, still on her feet and trying to evade his murderous whip. He stepped to her step and the whip cut through her bodice and ripped a deep furrow in her right tit. This spun her, and he snapped the neck of her dress, tearing the cloth down a full hand's length. All this before Frederick, seemingly frozen in the doorway, called, "Miss Marlene, Miss Marlene!"

He couldn't cut her down. With the speed of a striking snake, he sent the biting, tearing lashes to her struggling body, throat and breast, buttock and thigh. Her dress was in quick shreds and these were dyed with bold-red blood. But she would not go down and in fury, Jan wrapped the whip around one ankle and jerked with all his might. Tillie up-ended and went crashing to the flagstone floor. He laughed and cut her upraised hand nearly half through.

Now the fire was upon him. He forgot her lovely ass, her greedy, soft-lipped cunt and her softness under his powerful lust. He forgot all the intimate things she had ever said, and her soft laughter when he had reviled her stupid husband. He lost all memory of the greensward beside the wash creek and the twittering of the birds as he fucked her into whimpering delight. His whip sought bare flesh and he methodically whisked her dress away in critical places. The garment fell from her writhing body, exciting him to even greater frenzy. He cut her back in swift X-shaped patterns, then stroked her heaving belly with glee at her turning.

Back of him, he heard cries and shouts and a few pleas to him. He stole a moment to look at Frederick and some others, just untying the screaming actress. Sight of her naked beauty, now also lost to his cock, gave him fresh anger. He turned and stooped, his left hand tearing Tillie's skirt completely from her undernakedness. A hand gripped his coat from behind and he shrugged free. His whip tore the right lip from Tillie's cunt with a slushy popping sound. Her body stiffened in an arc of agony and he tore the other cunt lip from its bloody base. The body folded and rolled; he hated her tenacious clinging to consciousness and he sought her asshole. Once, twice he tore at the close-pressed cheeks of her ass, literally digging his way through her protective buttock to her vital anus. At each shrieking whistle of the whip, her frayed body gathered. Tillie had quit screaming through her mutilated mouth. Her torn hands seemed part of her torn face, the blood melted them together in one hideous distortion. Jan slowed his strokes, his desire to kill her giving way to his lust to hurt her to the point of giving sign.

She seemed to know that he wanted to tear her anus because she would not draw up her legs to bend her bottom for his pleasure. He cut her calves, her thighs and finally, her legs began to fold, jerking as agony and determination fought a hopeless battle. With saliva dripping from his smile, Jan leaned and sent the whip out in a long side-arm streak. The lash popped precisely at her bum hole, and blood leaped forward as if expelled from her bowel. Tillie seemed to leap from the floor, but it was only spasmodic anguish. She fell hard to the juncture of floor and wall and lay very still. Jan laughed bommingly and took a deep bite from first the right and then the left cheeks of her bloody, sagging ass. When she did not jerk or twitch, his rage became monumental. His cock, now very hard and lifted against his trousers, screamed for relief. His breath came fast but evenly and his mouth was clamped in rugged thinness. He wrapped the lash around one of Tillie's forearms and turned her to her back. Her legs flopped out, revealing her mutilated cunt, now a frayed mass of flesh and streaming scarlet. He tore the nipples, one at a time from her streaked and welted tits. He could not stop nor did he want to. Any small patch of unscarred white drove him to turn it red and halve it. He was not aware that all other sound in the cottage had ceased. He heared only the pop of his whip and the hiss of his own breath through his hairy nostrils. He lashed on, frenzied.

Somehow, she was standing, wrapped in the coverlet, between Malcomb Fageol and Frederick Tensington. She sensed other people in the one-room cottage, but her eyes were riveted to the way in which the terrible man was reducing Tillie to a shredded and bloody heap. Marlene fought for each breath, her brain so atrophied by what she witnessed it failed to instruct her lungs to function. Blood. It poured from Tillie's once magnificent body in gushes and small oozings, streaking her with garish patterns. The conquering whip was soaked with the thick lifefluid a full forearm's length from the biting fire-tongues at the tip. Blood spattered everywhere, on the floor, the wall and on Jan Macklin. The dying fire hissed as droplets landed amid the coals. Blood. Bits of flesh. Bits of passion never more to pulsate. Marlene remembered much, but it somehow had nothing to do with the devastated body on the stone floor. That was not anyone she had ever known. That was a lush female, being slowly reduced to a carcass by a man Marlene thought she remembered but she wasn't sure. He was beautiful, like a massive devil. His face was contorted with some emotion she did not understand. He seemed angry, but he seemed pleased. He was huge and powerful and had a handsome, if bloodspecked face. She thought she might like to be fucked by him when he tired of whip-fucking the woman over there. That was it, she decided. She wanted to be fucked by this giant of a demon. She wanted his prick in her mouth, in her cunt and up her bum hole, everywhere, just to absorb his furious jism in her aching body. She looked at the others in the cottage. They seemed equally in love with the big, whip-swinging man. The women, oddly familiar, were clutching one another, their hands in bodices and in skirt folds, and they seemed to roll and hunch in rhythm to the whistling whip. The men stood as if turned to stone, their eyes bugged out, their mouths hanging slackly from which tongues darted and licked. Marlene looked back at the body on the floor. It was jerking and twisting. It had no cunt; it had a hundred cunts, then it had a broad, beautiful ass, rapidly turning to scarlet pulp as the wonderful whip chewed at the prominent rounds. She envied the ass as the whip fucked its little rose to a gaping, gushing mouth. Fucked in the ass by a stick; it seemed to be a memory but Marlene couldn't still it in her turmoiled mind. Finally, she became so jealous of the still body on the floor that she could not stand the pain. She jerked and twisted free of the listless hands that supported her. With a high, shrill scream, Marlene leaped forward and hurled herself onto the still carcass. She buried her face in the bloody valley between the burst tits, praying for the bite of that glorious, whistling whip. It came, not as a bite but as a soft, slithering caress. She looked up at the demon who held the butt in his seemingly nerveless grip.

"Fuck me, fuck me, fuck me!" she hissed. "Oh, God! If you don't whip me I'll die, I'll die!"

A woman screamed. A man cried, "No!" Someone wailed.

Then the whip whistled again and Marlene had instant cum as the red line across her belly slowly began to ooze thick scarlet jism. Fascinated, she smeared the hot fluid with marveling fingers and her delighted laughter came in low, slow bubbling. Half leaning on the warm wet woman shape, Marlene spread her legs and drew them up, her bloody hand beckoning the slithering plaited snake to the bended beauty, hotly divided by her quaking quim in its nest of auburn hair. She hunched her belly to invite the lash.

Abruptly she seemed overwhelmed by hands and faces and she screamed protest as she was lifted from the floor. She kicked and flailed but the hands were cruelly insistent. "No, no, let it cut me, let it fuck me! No, I want—"

Then as she was held, hanging in the hard grip of men, another closed to her spraddled thighs and a prick rammed full into her cunt. She screamed, twisted and tried to draw away. The cock remained, and the panting man lopped his hands under her back and pulled her hard to his jolting groin. The force of his lust pushed all back, and Marlene's back was again on the hated bed. But she could not escape, the body over hers crushed firmly, only the swift hard undulations of cock seemed free. Wailing, Marlene felt herself responding to the plowing organ. She closed her eyes and guided the hips with her taut thighs. Her spine curled up, lifting to the ruthless pole and the hard bumping groin. It was not like the whip but it was excruciatingly good; she inhaled the hot, brandy laden breath burning down on her face and her hands went up to curl around the bowed neck, pulling the sweet rapist closer, deeper. She opened her eyes; she supposed the face belonged to Harvey or Alfred or Frederick or Adrian but it didn't matter. She fought to find the rhythm, the uphunch to meet the down thrust and presently the cock seemed to swell in her burning cunt, filling every aching space with sweet violence but somehow failing to satisfy the blazing desire. She speeded her fucking, wailing as the prick seemed to slow. She thought of all the working muscles in her belly and tried to force them into more furious gripping, and when the first hot spurt of jism hit the top of her cunt, she cursed and twisted in frustration. And then the body was gone, dragging the dripping cock from her hungry quim. She lay, still fucking with frenzied rolls and twists, her hands blindly groping to reclaim the exquisite prick. And she found it, stiff and fat and wonderfully long, and she scrooched her ass to meet the pulsing head as it lunged to her. Her lungs gave out a mighty gust of relief as the prick researed the inner lips and she met the plunging with all her strength. The face was different, the breath hotter; she clamped her legs around the body and clutched it hard to her crotch. The face didn't matter, it was the prick, the brutal, heavenly prick and she visioned it as a hungry snake, nibbling sharply at the raw and gleeful nerves in her screaming cunt. The madness, the need seemed to build, but the harder she fought for the sweet, all exploding moment, the further it floated from her grasp.

"The whip, the whip!" she screamed. "I must have the whip!"

It came, precisely to the underside of her straining thigh, its pop a beautiful bird song, its bite a showering agony that darted straight to join the bludgeon in her quim. Marlene shrieked her joy; the cum burst in her belly with myriad colors and rippled from head to toe in furious haste. She fought the lunging cock for its sweet jism and when it came, she felt it churn within her like a bath of fire. Then the cock was gone, and she lay, panting humping slowly, waiting for what she did not know until another cock was there, freshly fat and frenzied to burst her cunt.

Jan's head swirled, his eyes only half focused on the madness his whip had created. He had never known why he delighted in whipping a woman, or a horse, or even a cowering field hand, but he stood in the center of the room, the bloody whip hanging from his hand, his cock working smoothly in the pretty blonde girl's mouth, aware that his brutal murder of Tillie Fedren had triggered fantastic passions in the dozen undisciplined guests. On her hands and knees, a lush dark girl poised with her face but a few centimeters from Tillie's torn cunt, and the man who humped his prick into the dark girl's bum seemed hypnotized by the bloody spectacle so close in front. Like himself, every man in the room displayed a rampant peter, either pushing it to a laughing, hunching fluffy or standing in a sensate crouch, waiting for his turn at the insanely insatiable Marlene. She screamed again and without dislodging his prick from the girl's clinging mouth, sent the bloody lash to the milk white thigh of the actress. In response she clamped her arms and legs around Frederick and seemed to strain to his plunging organ as if unable to absorb enough. The sight made Jan's jism bubble up and out and his free hand held the blonde head while he rammed his cock into her throat so hard her mouth flew open in distress, leaking his cum from her scarlet lips in thick dribbles. He hurled her away, less interested in his prick than he'd thought possible. He swayed, and like an artist finishing a picture, sent his whip in small biting accuracy to an exposed buttock or a bouncing tit. The small cries and short yelps his artistry produced caused his blood to pump; his prick, dripping its last orgasmic drops, did not sag and weigh heavily. It stood, swaying and jerking as his mind toyed with greater lusts. He could not think, and he did not try. The single room, filled by thrusting, spreading bodies, lighted by the single lantern, seemed to Jan some sort of an exalter. When hot hands and an urging body came to him, he flung the woman aside with the sweep of his left arm. As she stumbled, he bit her bended ass with the lash and laughed as she screamed and rolled to tear at her long, conical tits as if in furious cum.

They were piling on the bed now. They had turned Marlene over to her hands and knees and the man who had begun this entire debacle was fucking the London beauty in the ass. Another was holding her head between spread hands, his cock coursing in her mouth in rhythm to the fucker in her rear. A third crowded close, hands fluttering from tits to balls and then to where the surging cocks entered the squirming body. Jan had no memory of when they had all disrobed, enough at least to free their flesh for the frenzied orgy. He saw only flouncing tits, bended buttocks and urging pricks. Faces blurred and he picked only the roundest forms and the tightest muscles for his targets. Then he saw the heavy whore, the ribald Anne, curled over Tillie's body, her face buried in the bloody crotch in animated seeking. He saw the woman's hands, feeling and pinching the torn tits, smoothing bloody patterns as she caressed the dead body in abandoned ecstasy. He cut the broad ass and his prick jerked as the woman instantly began to fuck at an imaginary prick. Lips drawn in an animal snarl, Jan moved forward on shaky legs and fell over the licking sucking woman, his cock digging at the massive darkness of her hair-surrounded cunt. He jabbed and jolted, and when he finally met the eager searching of her rump, he fucked into her with blind fury. She screamed and tried to evade the monstrous cock in her rectum and Jan reversed the whip butt in his hand and clubbed the rounded back and the thickly fatted shoulders with unreasonable rage. Finally, he backed his prick from her bum hole and hurled her aside.

On his knees, his shitty cock swaying, his breath coming in great gusts through his flared nostrils, he stared down at Tillie's carcass. The blood had ceased to flow, her heart was still. She was a scarlet woman, her body coated with her own blood, drawn to glorious gleaming by his God-whip. He stared harder, and as his senses reeled, he began to weep, not in sobbing grief, but in quiet dismay. Confused by the soft things he thought, Jan fell slowly forward, gathering the bloody, irresponsive body into his arms. His cock moved searchingly, and he found her lipless cunt. With more gentility than he had ever shown her in passionate life, he eased his cock into the lifeless cunt and urged it completely in.

"Sorry, bitch," he breathed to the blood-smeared face. Then he had the mightiest, most devastating orgasm of his life. He moaned and grunted as his jism streamed to the unfeeling vagina in seemingly endless spewing. Three, five, twenty times his balls knotted and his back twitched, and even when his prick was swimming in its own ejaculation, his blackly shrouded mind thought he could feel the familiar milk and suck of the cooling cunt. She was, as he had always said, the best fuck on the Tensington Estate. Then Jan rolled off of the body, to lie flat on his back, his eyes closed, his lips showing a strange yellow froth. Even in his spasm, his hand gripped the whip in massive claim.

Her face was to the rough sheet, her arms lay out and around the tangled mass of her hair. Her back sagged, causing the jism to flow from her belabored cunt and trickle down until it dropped to join the sticky splotch under her weary tits. Her knees seemed grown to the bed, the plunging cock in her up-reared ass barely shook her. Marlene whimpered with fire-pain, her down-head position made each beat of her heat sound as loudly as the grunts from the man clamped to her ass. The other sounds were dimming; it took her several seconds to identify the slush-slush as the one her asshole made as the prick pushed in and then retracted. It was good, the pumping feeling in her belly was almost a massage. The bump of groin to nates was a pleasant impact and occasionally, his swinging balls knocked to her inflamed cunt. She supposed her ass was delighted; two, three or five times, a steaming prick had plumbed its depths, sawing in and out to set the no-longer rubbery ring aflame. But she had not cum, not once since they had placed her in this ridiculous position and opened her rectum to their passions. She needed the whip, she needed the whip.

She moved her right arm, sending the fluttering hand back to the open wounds. Her fingers dug at the bloody encrustations, hoping to liven the pain, the sweet agony. She pretended the rustle of her fucker's knees on the bed was the whistle of the lashes and the grunt at the end of his lunge was the pop. She groaned at the uselessness of her game. The whip was gone. She tried another dream; she hung by her wrists, her naked body swaying as the lash turned and streaked her waist and bottom. Then the cock, the massive tree of life, thrust up from behind, spreading, ripping into her cunt with ruthless power. She pushed back to the pole in her rectum, she held her breath, hovering at the brink of the marvelous dive into purple bliss. It didn't do. Marlene sagged, weeping softly.

"The whip, the whip!" she moaned. "Fuck me with the whip! Jan, Jan! Oh God! I cannot stand this another instant!"

She toppled, slipping off the abruptly spurting prick. She felt the weak tap-tap on her thigh. Feeble spit from a weary mouth, a useless baptism. Marlene cried herself into blackness.

nine

When Jan awakened, he did not know where he was.
He still clung to the whip. It was very dark. His free
hand discovered the flagstone floor on which he lay,
then it moved to a blanket edge and as his fingers
crawled up over the irregular form it covered, he remembered.

Still addled, he climbed to his feet, discovering that
his breeches somewhat hobbled his movements. He
shivered. Laboriously, he found a sulphur match in his
pocket and snapped it to life on the hard edge of a
table. The flare half blinded him but he found the lantern. Then he stood in shock as his eyes swept the dev-

astated interior of the Fedren cottage. His own condition stunned him further. His cock was completely encrusted with blood, as was his belly. He had no memory of how he had come to such a state. Staggering, he moved to Tillie's rocking chair and slumped to a seat. Tillie.

He had cut her to death with his whip. He had torn her mouth from cheek to cheek so she could not protest her innocence nor even cry for mercy. Before the eyes of the jaded London fluffies and their perverted men, he had torn the best fucking woman he had ever known to bloody shreds. For Frederick, the Lord and Leader of the gruesome sons-of-stable-bitches. Jan swore, clearing his head a bit.

He needed no schoolmaster to tell him what had occurred after his mind had quit reveling in the gory orgy his whip had crea.ed.

Somehow, they had gathered their cocks and their cunts and what little wits they had salvaged and left the butcher's shop to him. He looked at the bed; its emptiness only emphasized the venal circus that had been there the last time he had looked. He snorted mirthlessly. They had saved the beautiful and famous Marlene de la Sage from the 'country woman,' all right. To fuck her cunt and bum until hardly a man could stand, while the blood of a better cunt soaked into the unfeeling flagstones in final cooling. Jan got up, steadied himself and went to the blanket-shrouded shape. He clamped his teeth, then pulled the blanket away.

His cock jerked at the beautiful destruction he had wrought. She lay in what seemed to be a comfortable sprawl, arms akimbo, legs widely out. Dried blood, nearly black, lay over her skin like a close fitting gown.

Her tits were slightly deflated, lying heavily in nippleless rounds across her ribcage. Her belly had also lost its normal curve and her hip bones showed like anchors for a slightly sagged creek bridge. He stared at her cunt, remembering how he had reformed its once pouting glory. Each bit of the whip was plain; the frayed edges of her skin stood stiff and ragged, and the inner tissues had shrunk away from her always throbbing clitoris, now only a ridge of nearly white gristle. Her cunt hole gaped; he had a brief flash of memory which eluded him quickly.

He spread the blanket then knelt to roll her onto it. For a moment, he couldn't believe his artistry in cutting out her bum hole. It showed as a ragged cavern, with blood and shit encrusted between the once magnificent nates. His nostrils flared at the smell of her carcass. With some reluctance, he covered her closely.

He went to the door, still hanging as he had left it after ripping it from the hinges. Outside, a faint gray signaled the approach of dawn. His mind settled. There was a gigantic job to do, one relegated to him by the trusting Frederick. While the fluffies and the fops soundly slept away their crimes, he was left with this. He ruffled his whip and swung it but there was no pop, no exciting snap. Half of it was stick-like with dried blood. It would take a thorough soaking, a careful drying and some warm tallow, he mused. Like himself, it had survived a massive ordeal with little damage.

The thought caused him pause. Perhaps not so slight a damage as he would have liked. A dozen of the gentry had seen him kill Tillie with his whip. A dozen fingers pointing, a dozen voices ridiculing the only story he could tell. They would stick together, just as they had rolled and fucked and sucked together in this very house. With that, there was the anguished story the beauteous Marlene could tell. He guessed her to be the most dangerous of them all because he had watched her scream and hump for cock at cunt and bum in excess of the others' rudest accommodations.

He went back and lifted the stiffened body of Tillie to the bed. He pulled the covers and pillowed her battered head. He had the urge to fuck her, but the flesh under his hands was cold and hard. For a moment, he fought the recurrence of the dizziness that had afflicted him since awakening. Then he took down the lantern, shook it to verify its half-full reservoir, and with no hesitation, crashed it to the floor beside the bed. He had to leap to escape the instant billow of red-black flame. He moved to the door, watching the tongues of flame creep to every corner of the cottage. When he last looked, the bed on which Tillie lay was a mass of flaming bedclothes.

Striding heavily, his huge body outlined by the light of the blossoming fire, he walked up the hill and made his way to his own cottage. At this hour, on the Sabbath, the house would burn to sullen ashes before any Tensington serf would even smell the smoke.

Malcomb Fageol stood at the stone rail of the second floor terrace and watched the sky come alive with red-gold flame. The dawn showed the smoke as a darker trail in the overcast sky. He shuddered, because this night had been the worst of his remembering.

He alone, had seemed to retain enough sense to know when the orgy had ended. One by one, he had straightened them up and headed them up the path to the manse, ignoring their gibberish and silencing their hysterical laughter. Frederick had recovered enough to help him lift Marlene from her bath of jism and half-carry, half-drag her to the manse. Then had come the task of sorting the disheveled guests to their proper bed-chambers. After that, he had bathed Marlene and anointed her whip bites.

He leaned on nerveless hands, his mind incapable of fully understanding what had happened. His skin crawled as he remembered his own unreasonable excitement as the groundskeeper had begun the systematic end of the woman known as Tillie Fedren. He, like the others, had succumbed to the passion of violence, the brutality of a beast. There was no doubt in his mind that the fire a kilometer distant was the Fedren cottage, and that the mutilated body was already toasted beyond recognition. He cursed himself for being a fool; had he thought to set fire to the carnal house himself, the groundskeeper would no longer be a threat. He could not ignore his fear of the man. At a word and a look from Frederick, Jan Macklin had ripped the country lesbian to shreds. Later, he had stood like a colossal satyr, his massive cock in mouth and cunt, limp cunt at that, and his whip as solid in his fist as if it had grown there. And now, the fire and smoke from the gully testified again to the man's inhuman command of the situation.

Malcomb shuddered. No one had bothered to make sure that Tillie Fedren had been dead. Had Macklin, he wondered? And would he have cared or changed his plan of disposal if there had been a heartbeat or a diminutive breath? Malcomb thought not; he was too weak a man to question the ruthlessness of stronger souls. Weary beyond expression, he went back to his room, a cold, lonely cubicle of stone. When he blew out his lamp, the darkness crushed in upon him like a vengeant beast. He gave a yelp of terror and leaped into bed, quivering like a small child who could see spectres in the dark.

———————————

The sun was coming over the hedgerows when they came for him. Frederick, still drugged by sleeplessness, donned his clothes and followed the excited man. As they half-ran toward the gully path, Frederick saw the fading feather of smoke, and if at first he did not understand, he did when he saw Jan Macklin, also partially dressed, standing among the dozen awed farmers who had gathered at first alarm. Frederick drew a massive sighing breath as he saw how the cottage was only a mound of smoldering ashes, the stone walls cracked and tumbled so only the fireplace remained in uprightness. The heat was terrific but at Jan's shoulder, he moved close enough to see into the dying holocaust.

"Where is Tillie Fedren?" Frederick asked.

Jan turned and in a voice guaranteed to carry to the farmers, replied: "In her bed, or what is left of it, sir, I imagine. As you know, her husband, Joseph, is in Watertown and her daughter is serving your guests in the manse. It would seem poor Tillie went to sleep with the lantern going, or had some accident if she had dozed and arose in half-sleep to turn it down. Ah, a fine woman! Joseph will be devastated! Oh, did any of you send for the parish priest?"

There were nods and a man admitted that he had sent

his son to bring the Father. Frederick, much relieved, saw fit to make a small speech about the sorrow he felt at such a disaster. He set the onlookers about bringing buckets to utilize the creek water to cool the sad remains. Then he walked with Jan back toward the manse.

"I cannot say you fool, Jan Macklin," he said. "I only hope the rest of the mess cleans itself as readily! Have you any idea exactly what happened there last night?"

"No, sir, I have not," came the steady reply.

"I see. I'm sure it will always remain a complete mystery. I am also sure that this tragedy will somewhat dampen the festive spirits of my guests. They are immensely sensitive people."

"That is undoubtedly true, sir."

"Yes. Well, I think I should alert the stables to the possibility of a mass exodus today, groundskeeper. And I should like a special carrier for Miss Marlene. As a dedicated artist of great responsiveness, she will unquestionably be very upset. I might even suggest that you, yourself, drive her carriage to London, as a favor to me and to her."

"Do you think, sir, that she will be comfortable in the company of a mere groundskeeper?"

"Ah, your insight is excellent. However, I am sure she will be accompanied by Mister Fageol, rather a competent gentleman in the management of difficult ladies. She may not even notice you, Jan."

"I surrender to your judgment, sir."

Frederick nodded. His wits, not fully alert, itemized the seriousness of the situation. He thought of offering the groundskeeper some mild concession, or even a few pound notes, but his arrogance interfered, at least until some indication of more acute danger occurred. He had, he thought, only to raise his finger and the magistrate would sentence Jan Macklin to the hangman's noose. Then he shivered. In appearing as he had, with words of condolence for Tillie Fedren, and not one word of scold nor accusation for the groundskeeper, Frederick had forever nullified any chance of later hurling blame and vilification on Jan Macklin. He was trapped as an accomplice in whatever developments might be brought to light.

Then, because he was not a man of great courage, Frederick glanced sideways at the larger man. He wore the whip coiled over his left shoulder, but it was not the regular plaited one, the deadly instrument that had killed Tillie and turned his guests into frantic, lusting animals. It was slimmer and darker, and apparently longer. But it was a whip and in the hands of a man like Jan Macklin, any length of line was a coercive device. It spelled death, destruction and demanded surrender. Moreover, by giving Jan the privilege of using his talented whip, he might be granting the strange man the very concession that would keep him firmly in subservience.

"Ah. I anticipate a change of plans, groundskeeper," he said as they reached the manse. "I would guess that my guests will be up and about by nine-thirty, ten at the latest. As you are better equipped to calm their apprehensions over the unfortunate accident to Tillie Fedren, I might like to have you present when I give them the sad news. Is this an idea of any merit?"

Jan's chuckle was unnerving to Frederick. "Yes, sir. I guess I do have a calming effect on excited people! Say, at ten, sir?"

Frederick smiled and patted the groundskeeper's thick arm. "Ten will be perfect. And I may let you break the sorrowful news to Mary Fedren. Would that be to your liking?"

"No, sir, it would not! All other things you have suggested, but not that task, if I may be so bold!"

Frederick wilted inside. "All right, groundskeeper, I'll manage the task myself. At ten, then."

Marlene knew she was awake but she was afraid to open her eyes lest Tillie would be there, staring down with the peculiar hunger in her eyes. She was also afraid to move because even a small, careless movement would torture her raw wrists and rope-bruised ankles. She was surprised that she had slept so soundly while her naked body throbbed with pain and her distorted muscles ached with such intensity. Then she felt a strange softness under her head, not at all like the lumpy pillow Tillie had stuffed in place to ease the tensions in her neck. And the cover over her was softer than the rough blanket she had learned to love, if not for its warmth and gentility, for its covering of her blatant nudeness. She chanced a small movement of her hips; the broomstick was gone but her rectum felt as if it had been impaled by a tree. There was an emptiness in her stomach, but it didn't seem like hunger. She shivered. Her body was finally free of rough intrusions and scalding insertions. Slowly, she turned her head and prepared to open her eyes and face another day of degradation, humiliation and worst of all, surrender to the insidious crawling need in her body, so easily excited by the unabashed Tillie.

Then her eyes popped fully open. With a gasp, she squirmed to one elbow. Her wrists were not tied, nor were her feet. She could not believe the familiarity of the room in which she lay, nor the elegance of her bed and the closely drawn drapes of weighty velvet. She held up her arm searching for the roughness at the willowy wrist. It seemed to be there, but there was no circlement of scarlet. She threw back the covers and drew up one tapered leg. Her yelp of agony caused her to fall back before she could inspect her ankle. Her hips were brutally stiff, almost immobile. She felt the sharp pains under her thighs and then one across her belly. Her eyes widened in disbelief. The slightly scabbed wound was as long as her hand and it began, or ended, she did not know, with a positive pit in her skin. Gingerly, she felt of the wounds in her thigh and buttock. They were of the same character, longer or shorter, but all possessing a massive soreness. She whimpered in confusion, and finally admitted the soreness at other places. She bended and looked at her cunt, shocked by its difference. The lips were dark and swollen and they thrust out as if to seek cooling air and gentle massaging. Her groin was clean, but the hair had a basic sticky feeling when she ran her fingers through it. Not until later did she run her fingers down and under to test her bum hole. It was swollen, puckered and throbbing. She relaxed in trembling memory. It had not been a dream. It had been a very real horror, beginning with her strange adventure at the hands of the groundskeeper, the handsome one, and ending, somehow, with her massive degradation at the hands of Tillie Fedren. Marlene moaned as memories tumbled into clarity. She flushed as she recalled how her fear of Tillie, and Tillie's philosophies had melted into total acquiesence. She squirmed as she recalled the furious ecstasies the country woman's hands and lips had induced, and she hated herself as she re-visioned her own assault upon the wonderful delight of Tillie's crotch. She licked her lips and swallowed, almost tasting the acrid oozings of Tillie's cunt. She stared at her right forefinger, clean now, but once so sweetly browned from its adventure in the palpitating asshole of her lewd guardian.

Trying to hasten through her memories, Marlene came to a bulwark; she remembered the furious agony, following massive delight, of the broom handle in her rectum. Enthralled by not to be forgotten agony, she shifted her wounded ass and it was almost as if she could feel the deep impalement again. Then she remembered Tillie's fury, generated because she had been called a foul slut. Marlene winced at the stab of the straw broom, and from there, she seemed unable to remember.

But she lay now, quivering with residual terror, safe and warm and harassed by no physical threat. It had all been some foul game, instigated by Frederick Tensington or the handsome, brutal Jan. Jan Macklin. She recalled the intensity of Tillie's words about the near-giant. The descriptions of his prick, which Marlene had felt but hardly seen. The tales of fuck and suck beside the gully creek. The weary recital of submission to cruel violence, followed by the confession that no woman could resist the mighty stud. A poor soul, Tillie, uneducated, amoral and the victim of her lowly position in the scheme of Tensington affairs. Marlene sighed.

It had been pure terror but it was over. She had survived the senseless ordeal because she was morally strong and aloof to the vagaries of the ungentle. Today was Sunday; by mid-afternoon she would be on her way back to London and the realities of a saner world. She had a qualm because she knew nothing about jism or the effects of it in her quim. She clung to the certainty that God would not permit Jan Macklin's cum to impregnate her innocent ovaries.

And because she was young and thrilled by her present freedom, she began to guess at her future. She had never really delighted in virginity or the posture of untouchability maintained throughout her seven or eight adult years. She was famous, talented and loved by multitudes; it had always been a burden to refuse the ultimate in adoration, the physical enactment of a handsome swain's devotion. Frederick, poor hysterical man, had taken care of the troublesome maidenhead and taught her the delights of a plunging prick. If she had wept and protested, she had yet felt the deep inner growth from adolescent to adult, from foolish, idealistic girl to woman. Marlene giggled. If being raped had reaped such illicit pleasures, what might she enjoy in moments of conscious love? Shocked by her mental gymnastics, she stilled, and her mind tumbled, as if trying to insert memories she could not recall into her present glee over freedom.

They were peculiar memories, of blood and fury and frenzy, but she couldn't solidify them and finally gave up in disinterest.

"Oh, dear me!" she gasped, suddenly realizing that her hand had wandered down to the pulsating nest between her thighs, and that the soreness was prohibitive to the unconscious action of her fingers. But it excited her to realize that a part of her beautiful body never before admitted, had come alive with such positive reactions. She even made excuses for Frederick Tensington. He was a handsome man of property, position and worldly experience. How could he have known that she was a virgin, innocent of body and mind when her friends were obviously of a less restricted nature? She giggled; she had driven him half out of his mind and he had fucked her violently while she still lay half-embraced by her ridiculous corset.

Presently however, Marlene began to doubt herself. Frederick had hurled her over the edge of the cliff; Jan Macklin had beat her down into even deeper depths. Seemingly, a massive conspiracy had deprived her of every moral standard, piling degradation and humiliation upon until she had now awakened, sore, abused and of a mind she had never before believed possible. She shuddered. Even if she casually remembered the way a rampant penis looked as it sought her body and attentions, her belly tightened and her spine tingled. How could she ever face another cock without succumbing to the throes of memory and delight?

So she sat up, ignoring her aching asshole and her stinging wounds. By some quirk of fate, she had fallen among beasts, and if their pleasures were contagious, she would fight the temptations with a basic purity and mental chastity. She began to cry softly, not sure of herself at all. A pain in her belly she had ignored became very oppressive. She longed desperately for a script to recite with a director to explain her faults and applaud her victories.

Lydia stood at the foot of the short flight of stairs rising to the closed door of the small chapel, long since converted into a special chamber for Master Tensington's special guests. Down the corridor, Gibson seemed preoccupied in counting silver at an open cupboard. And when his nod came, Lydia hurried up the six steps and hastily fitted the tarnished brass key Gibson had given her. The lock snapped loudly, giving Lydia the shivers. Then she was inside the rather large room. Mary Fedren was standing by a grilled window. She turned and smiled.

"Oh, Lydia! You've come to take me home!" she cried, and with a peculiar, limping gait, came toward the maid. Lydia met her with a gentle arm around the slim shoulders.

"No, dear. But something dreadful has happened and I thought it best I come explain to you as best I could. Now, there's a dear. Sit down and listen carefully."

"I can not go home to my mama?" Mary asked with concern.

"No, Mary. But not for the reasons you might think."

It had seemed like a simple, straightforward story the way she and Gibson and Wife Medwick had agreed it should be told to Mary, but with the child's blue eyes so squarely meeting her, the story began haltingly and became quite hysterical. Mary seemed not to hear until Lydia came to the end of the gruesome tale by explaining that they had found the remains of her mother's body in the ashes of her bed. There had just been a terrible accident which no one knew anything about. Mary lowered her quivering chin.

"Mama is dead, then, isn't she?"

"Oh, you poor darling!" Lydia exclaimed, bursting into tears as she claimed the slender form with her round firm arms. "Oh Mary!"

She was surprised at the way Mary twisted free of the embrace and sat, staring down at the floor. The child seemed stunned, which Lydia thought was natural, yet there was a pout to her lips that was not petulance. Her small jaw was clamped in apparent determination to not cry, although her eyes were swimming. Lydia thought Mary was the bravest little girl she had ever known.

"I am so sorry, Mary," she murmured. "I hate to go away and leave you now, but if Master Tensington knew I'd come to tell you of the tragedy, he'd skin me! I'm sure he'll be about to tell you himself but he is distraught and very tired, having all those guests and being up at the first news of the fire. Now, curl up and have a good cry and I'll bring your breakfast as soon as the master comes with the proper key. Poor, dear darling. But we will all take care of you until your daddy returns from Watertown."

"Go away."

"Mary!"

Shocked and confused, but still remembering the precariousness of her position, Lydia got up and went to the door. Mary neither looked nor waved good-bye. She walked in her limping way to the window and looked out into the overcast gray of morning. Sobbing for some reason she did not understand, Lydia slipped out of the room, relocked the door, then went scurrying to Gibson for condolence.

Gasping and trembling, Lydia told the gray-haired

major-domo of Tensington about Mary's strange reactions. His face did not change expression throughout her rather incoherent report. When she blubbered to silence, he gave her a second brutal shock.

"Go about your work and keep your bloody mouth shut, wench," he said. "I will manage what else should be done."

Again Lydia broke into brief tears; it seemed to her that no one in the world had real deep feelings about anything or anybody.

ten

With some flare for the dramatic, as well as a deep apprehension for what lay ahead, Frederick had sent Gibson around to the guests with an invitation to meet at ten in the upper parlour. Now, as he entered the room, he perceived that it was going to be easier than he'd guessed. They were a very haggard looking lot, with worried faces and in twos and threes, and when he entered the room, with the arrogant and unsmiling Jan at his shoulder, they turned frightened eyes to him and fell silent.

"Good morning, all," Frederick said, trying to maintain his calm. "I brought you here this morning to

break a rather bad bit of news. It has nothing to do
with any of you, of course," he added. "It is just that
the pallor of grief hangs over Tensington today and I
felt required to inform you of the facts rather than to
let rumor and country gossip startle you. The facts are
these. Sometime just before daylight, the house of one
of my tenants caught fire and burned to the ground before anyone was alarmed to the tragedy. The poor
woman, Tillie Fedren, who was alone in the cottage was
burned to death in her bed. No one knows how the fire
started nor why she was unable to excape its fury. At
any rate, my groundskeeper, Jan Macklin, has investi-
gated the matter and I have brought him here in case
you—any of you—have curiosities or concerns you'd
like settled."

"My God!" Harvey Samborne gasped.

Anne Grange rose half out of her chair, mouth
agape, eyes wide with horror. Then she sank back
slowly, her superior voluptuousness shaking visibly.
Frederick cast his eyes about the startled guests, paus-
ing no longer on Marlene de la Sage's stunned coun-
tenance than on any other. But she demanded attention.

"Tillie—Tillie is dead?" she asked in a strained voice.

"Yes, my dear, Macklin?"

Jan stepped forward. Over his shoulder was coiled
his favorite whip, sleek and freshly oiled. "Yes, Miss
Marlene," he said with even tenor. "Once the coals had
cooled, I was able to determine that her bones lay in
her own bed, definitely proving that she had been sound
asleep when the fire surprised her."

"You fiend!" someone whispered.

There was no indication of who had hissed the accusation.

It was Malcomb Fageol who stood then, his face bland. "A terrible thing, Frederick, I'm sure. I think we all thank you for giving us this opportunity to understand. You were quite right. It would have been a startling rumor to have heard at breakfast. In light of its tragic nature and its certain impact upon your people, should we all consider an early departure for London as the discreet thing to plan?"

"It is a matter for each to determine," Frederick said. He tried a smile to them all, and his nerves sang pleasantly at the ease of apparently settling the matter among the guests. They would gather and buzz and exchange remembering, but he was very sure that each felt a monumental guilt for the occasion, and each was selfish enough to welcome his explanation of Tillie Fedren's death. Particularly, with Jan standing by, seemingly unconcerned about his part in the entire affair. If there was a problem, it was Marlene's obvious confusion. She approached him now, with furtive glances at the stolid groundskeeper.

"Frederick, I must talk with you!" she husked. "I must!"

"But of course, my dear," he said, patting her shoulder. "Come with me. The groundskeeper and I have some important things to discuss, the services, the burial, and of course, the welfare of Tillie Fedren's husband and child. Do come to my quarters. It will be private there and you may be at ease."

"Oh, I've never been so terribly shocked before in my life!" Marlene murmured. "There is so very much I don't understand!"

This puzzled Frederick but he felt better about it when Jan fell into step behind as he led Marlene to his apartment. She was obviously very disturbed but he couldn't fathom her apparent pretense at innocence. She acted to Frederick as if she had been genuinely surprised by his announcement of Tillie's death. At his room, he opened the door and continued to escort her to a seat in his private sitting room, leaving the door to Jan. When Marlene sank to a seat, she saw the groundskeeper standing like a giant, his coiled whip now in his right hand. She gasped.

"I want to talk to you—without his presence, Frederick," she said. "In my eyes, he is a man of evil! I have suffered intolerable indignities at his hands. And that whip!!"

"Step to the other chamber, will you, groundskeeper?"

"I think not, sir. As a freeman, I have the right to hear any specific charges the lady may make, begging her pardon, and her words indicate a rather poor opinion of me! I am dismayed!"

"You are a brutal fiend, a rapist and a degenerate!" Marlene spat him. "Oh, Frederick, I am so confused I cannot think!"

"Calm yourself, my dear and start from the beginning. Would a brandy help your nerves and composure?"

She waved a gracious refusal. Frederick was more confused than she could possibly claim to be. If she had had no part in Tillie's death, she had still become, at the sight of violence and blood, the most avariciously avid example of sexual abandon he had ever known. He could still see her, fucking one man after another clutching at them in frantic eagerness. He could remember her wails, "—fuck me, fuck me, fuck me with the whip!" and how she had turned up her bum and cried with ecstasy as cock after cock had plumbed her ass, cried for more and more around the plunging pricks in her mouth.

"That animal!" she said, nodding to Jan. "All right, if I must state my case before him, I shall! There is no humiliation I have not already suffered at his hands— nor for that matter, at your hands, Frederick Tensington! You I may forgive partially because you are a man of gentle blood and I had voluntarily put myself in a deceptive position. But the rest of the story, you can not know!"

"I am distraught at your anger, my dear. Please, tell me what I do not know and I shall use every power at my command to rectify the hurts you have suffered."

And she began by confessing her attempt the previous morning to escape back to London. He pretended great surprise and let her talk. When she described the ordeal in the groundskeeper's cottage, he glared at Jan, hiding his subtle wink to the man with a turned head. Both men listened as she haltingly described in genteel terms, her treatment at the hands of the deceased country woman. She continued to remake in no uncertain terms, that it had been Jan who had turned her over to the insane woman. But as she carried her narrative to a near end, Frederick noted how her coherence faltered and how her account seemed to skip from horror to horror without continuity. And when she slowed to a near whisper in her remembering, he looked at Jan with a quizzical eye. Jan shrugged.

"Oh, I am confused!" she finally said. "The last I remember was lying on the bed, tied hand and foot, my body a mass of bruises and my mind buffeted by terror.

The woman, Tillie Fedren, had become angry over my revilement of her savagery. She had struck me violently and degraded me with—with a broom handle! This morning, I awakened in my own room, in my own bed. I know not how I got there, nor what had happened in the interim! But my body testified to the certainty that I had survived all I have told you. Oh, dear God, what have I done?"

"You, my dear?" Frederick purred, patting her bowed shoulders. "I think you have been very brave, very strong. What do you think you have done?"

"Oh, Frederick, I do not know! But apparently, I was the last person to see Tillie Fedren alive! Could I have, by some inverted miracle, freed myself and—and overcome poor Tillie? Who knows what I did, my mind darkened by pain and fright, my instincts shattered and desperation my only strength? Frederick, Tillie was not a careless woman nor one of wandering wits! The lantern hung high and very firmly on its iron hook. If it had crashed to the floor and set fire to the cottage, it had to have human inspiration. Oh God, my heart shrivels at the thought of what human inspiration it might have been! I—I hated Tillie, in a way, but only an insane woman would burn another human being to death!"

Frederick looked over her sobbing form and grinned at Jan.

The groundskeeper winked in massive conspiracy.

"Well, now, my dear, we will never know, will we?" Frederick murmured. "And I think your guilt can remain a secret among the three of us—we all have transgressions to count, and hold privately. With that, you must not concern yourself unduly about the likes of

Tillie Fedren! She was, if your memory is precise, a woman of no moral fiber, aside from being a rather poor sort in a country way. There, there. I assure you that my tongue is sealed forever and the groundskeeper is a man of consummate honor. I will get you a brandy. Rest a bit and I will send a girl to help you pack for your immediate return to London. A tragic weekend, I'm sure, but one best forgotten with alacrity. Poor, dear Marlene! Life seems even more dramatic than the plays in which you lead, does it not? There, there!"

"You won't be needing me, I think, sir," Jan suggested.

"No. Go about your regular duties, groundskeeper."

"You—you are not going to punish him for what he d-did to me?" Marlene asked then.

Frederick smiled gently. "I would say we all have arrived at a point where retribution is best ignored in such matters."

———————————

She shed only two big tears, one spilling from each of her quiet blue eyes as she surveyed the pile of blackened stones and ashes. Frederick, holding the reins of the pony cart, put his free arm around Mary's shoulders, not because he shared her silent grief but because he felt very good. At this hour of the afternoon, his guests had all departed, including Marlene de la Sage, in company with Malcomb Fageol, carefully instructed about not trying to revive memories that Marlene seemed unable to generate, and driven by Jan Macklin, with further instructions about handling any unpleasant situations that might arise.

"Poor Mama," Mary murmured. "And Papa will be so sad!"

"Yes," Frederick agreed, his fingers softly molding the roundness of her small shoulder. "Life has it wounding, Mary. But as when I lost my own dear father, the grief passes and we must make our way to brighter things. Would you like to return to the mansion now? I expect you are very tired, are you not?"

"No. No. I am all right. But there is something I would like to do, Master Tensington."

"Oh? And what is that?" he asked, smiling down at her.

"A little farther, there is another path that leads down to the creek. It is to a place that Mama and I came every week to wash. I love the place very much because it was always so green and nice. Could we just visit it now? Mama and I enjoyed that place so much!"

"But of course," Frederick agreed. He plucked the buggy whip from the socket. It felt strangely substantial in his hand, even though its butt was not plaited and its single lash was but a meter of trimmed rawhide. He popped the pony's rump and the cart jerked forward. He still held Mary in his right arm.

"You must tell me where to turn, Mary," he said.

"Oh, yes. It is a bit farther, Master Tensington."

Presently, she pointed and he turned the pony with a sharp jerk. He was enthralled by the density of the gully woods, and his arm around Mary tightened to hold her close to his side. When they came to the creek bordered by the small area of greensward, he saw the flat stones that had been used for generations by farm wives.

"Here?"

"Yes sire, Would you help me out? I might wade a bit."

Her gait was awkward. Frederick lounged on the
short grass, flicking at flying things with the whip, but
mostly, watching Mary. She held her skirt well up above
the knees and with unsteady steps, moved out into the
stream. His eyes devoured the smoothness of her beginning thighs and he made out the form of her small
ass under the drawn skirt. His cock throbbed as his
mind, freed of the past day's worry, stripped the slim
body of its poor garments. In another year, that ass
would broaden and thicken and the fine pads of her
little breast shapes would bulge and bloom into lovely
tits. His cock did a small straightening jerk in his
trousers. Then she was tumbling, her bad hip failing.
She screeched as she fell forward into the water, then
came to her hands and knees in the shallow water,
laughing at her plight. She finally regained her feet and
the wet dress clung to her body with the faithfulness of
his memory. She waded ashore.

"Oh dear, I am so very wet!" she exclaimed, her
hands smoothing from breast to middle thigh in pressing the water from the cloth.

"Yes," he breathed. "Why don't you remove your
clothes and spread them there in the sun to dry?"

She looked at him and giggled. "All my clothes?"

"They are all wet, aren't they?"

She nodded. Frederick's head whirled as she began
to lift and tug her dress upward. He followed the rising
hem, delighting in the slender legs that moved into bare
encasement in her soaked bloomers, now hugging her
hips and bottom with amazing truth. He watched in
fascination as she hobbled to a sunlit bush and spread
her dress. In so doing, she stood with feet apart for
stability and bended. His cock stiffened painfully and

he moved it with nervous fingers, to lie up against his belly. Then he watched her skin out of her bodice and the fact of her youth was driving home by the flatness of her tits with the nipples sharp from the cold water. She looked over her shoulder at him and giggled. Then she worked her bloomers down and down, bending to pull the clinging wet cloth from her ankles. When she was naked, she turned and walked toward him, humped a bit to ease the catch in her hip. He saw the little cunt like a tailor's buttonhole, barely fringed with light blonde fuzz and only a shade pinker than her skin. He sat up, one hand outstretched to her.

"You are very pretty naked," he said. "Come, let me kiss you and adore your beauty!"

"No," she said. "It is not fair. I am naked and you are wearing clothes! If you would take off your clothes, Master Tensington, we might go into the water together. It is not really cold!"

"A fine idea!" Frederick replied. He came to his feet, his eyes still burning into her slender, immature crotch. He divested himself of his jacket, then his shirt, and finally, his trousers, boots and stockings. His prick was gigantic, swaying, lifting and jerking from his hairy groin and when he looked at Mary, she was staring as hard at his penis. To test her, he stroked his cock in foreskin release and she giggled at the manner of his prick's antics.

"I think it wants to fuck, does it not?" she asked.

"Ah, Mary, Mary!" he exclaimed and she moved into his crouched embrace. Her fingers went to the long, thickening member and as he mashed his mouth to her neck and cheek, she frigged him awkwardly. His hands sought her bottom, cupping the small nates and urging er to him so his cock rubbed against her belly with delightful kissing. Weak with desire, Frederick sank back to the grass, pulling her down with him, to kneel between his lean, out-flung legs.

She seemed fascinated by his up-standing cock and the lazy sack of balls hanging over his bum. She licked her lips in nervous attention, her fingers went to his cock and began to frig it, working the foreskin in a fine, excited slipping. Then to his surprise, she leaned down and closed her childish lips over his prick head. He frowned; it had not been anything he'd taught her during his first exquisite evening with her. But she bathed his glans with saliva and began to work her head up and down, her lips pursed firmly, as adeptly as any woman he had ever known. He trembled, feeling the rasp of her small tongue and his passions mounted rapidly. Her fingers now toyed with his balls, feeling of them as if they were fine cloth. He hunched slightly, sending his prick deep into her throat. She coughed.

"Oh, it tastes so delightful, Master Tensington! I fear what I do is very naughty, but it so fits my mouth I cannot resist it!" Her head dropped again, and he sent his cock into her mouth with a grunt and a hump. Excited beyond expectations, he bowed up and without freeing her lips, roughly turned her body, moving her legs to straddle his chest. The small ass spraddled, the deep crease between her little cheeks opened to expose her anus, a dark red circlet of mobile flesh just above the end of her fat-formed quim. He had to bring his head forward, her body being shorter than his, to lick and kiss into the delectable under-shapes. "Oh!" she gasped.

Frederick's mind nearly departed as his tongue found

the flavor of her cunt and plumbed the soft depths of its smallness. His prick in her mouth seemed to swell beyond reason, and he settled to fuck up into her lips with excruciating joy. Now her ass was rolling and grinding down as his tongue found and flicked the undeveloped clitoris. She squirmed and twisted, the frenzy traveling from his furious mouth to hers, and he panted into the small ass and planned eagerly to surprise her with his jism. When it spewed, she jerked up her head and coughed again. He hunched into air, but the moment was enough. She did not turn aside; his cum pumped against her face and she mewled with childish pleasure. Frederick bit fiercely at the open, saliva dripping cunt and her protest turned to laughter as she crawled around and put her dripping mouth to his. He tasted his own jism, sticky, musky and oddly sweet. His still throbbing prick lay up against her cunt and she squirmed appreciatively.

"You vixen!" he panted. "Ah, Mary, you must be mine forever! I can never let you go as long as I have life to spend in your body!"

"Oh. Oh, Master Tensington! I can hardly breathe!"

"A moment, Mary," he pleaded, feeling his prick weaken in her crotch. "Rub down on me—it will get hard very soon!"

"Will you fuck me with it, Master Tensington? I beg of you?"

"Yes, yes, yes! Until you cry for respite!"

His fingers under her rump felt the way her cunt lips lay open and partially around his cock at half girth. He found her anus and massaged it into sweet relaxation. Then he made to move her down so he could get the swollen head of his prick into the tiny slit.

"No, no," she murmured. "I cannot! Riding you so, my leg pains me greatly! Oh, I must——"

He helped her up, his prick aching to enter the receding nest. She crouched for a moment, panting, rubbing her hip joint but not turning out of his grasp.

"It is better now."

"There are other ways."

"Yes, how, how?"

He climbed to his feet, spreading them wide apart. Then he turned her and bent over, forcing her to bend. His prick lay hard to her bowed back so he wrapped his arms under her slim torso and lifted her, carrying her slight weight easily. "Spread your legs for a moment, my dear," he husked and when she did, he fitted her crotch to his, the whole length of his prick sliding into her saliva-lubricated cunt. She giggled and let her legs hang as he began to swing her to his hard stroking. That half his cock was loved by her inner thighs was of no consequence; he could feel the head of his organ opening and distending her vagina and her efforts to fuck him back were acutely telling. He had forgotten the feel of Mary's cum, but when her moaning explained itself to him, he continued to fuck, not able to meet her tiny spasms with his building jism. Her arms hung, her head was turning from side to side and he ignored the quaver of his knees in an effort to load her gulping quim with his fluids. He was deaf to her panting, her squirming was all he needed, and as his tight arms caused her to twist for breath, the screwing motion made his prick seem raw and he clutched her up to ram his cum into her deepest cavity. So absorbed in her was he that his swaying turned to tumbling as the last spurting churned into her vagina. His knees went slack, he tumbled and they went down to the grass, grunting, laughing and scrambling together. Frederick lay flat, Mary a gleeful heat between his thighs. His cock lay over on his groin, dribbling gray-white fire as his balls gave their final urging. Then she had it in her hand, flopping its weight to rid the eye of its last drops. Frederick closed his eyes, so totally ecstatic he could hardly breathe.

"Have we tired you, Master Tensington?" Mary asked.

"No. No, Mary! But my poor cock needs a moment in which to find its strength. No! I will fuck you as often and as hard as you may want! I love you dearly!"

"I want it now," she said, stripping his prick from balls to tip, finishing the caress with a sprightly kiss. "I want it in my back place, but not like before, please, Master Tensington! I cannot lie on my back and spread my legs so again. My hip—"

"I am sorry for that, Mary," Frederick said.

"It will be fine, Master Tensington. But I want to fuck with my bum hole! Perhaps, like this?"

She was on her hands and knees at his side then, her small ass slightly opened because of her parted knees. Frederick stared at her dribbling cunt, and as he stared, she reached under and with lewdly delightful fingers, smeared his jism up over her asshole. She worked the sticky fluid in, herself entering the ringlet with a small finger. The demand was so voluble Frederick gasped. His weary cock jerked and flopped as blood began to pour into its listlessness. He came to his knees behind Mary, working his prick with frantic fingers, as if the beautiful little ass would evaporate in the evening warmth.

"Hurry, hurry, Master Tensington!" Mary pleaded. "Oh, my bottom is on fire for a fuck there! Oh, hurry and put it in me!"

Frederick cursed the lethargy of his cock. He squeezed it fiercely and stretched it and flopped it until it pained him. He leaned forward and rubbed the rubbery tube to her ass, exploring the shapes as if to educate his stupid flesh. And finally, his fingers were rewarded with a throb, and as he panted and hunched, his cock began to swell and distend. When it was barely firm, he put the head to Mary's asshole and tried to force it in. It mushroomed and slipped and he cursed again. Using a rough finger, he tried to open the little rectum and tuck the reluctant flesh into her. He was sweating and panting and his body vibrated with the strain of his efforts.

And eventually, his prick did stiffen and did enter her loosened bum. She reared back, and as his cock oozed slowly in, stretching the tiny rosebud into a strained white ring, he began to fuck as if driven by massive springs. He gripped Mary's hips in brutal hands and undulated with all the power of his weary back. The little body, the distorted anus and the moans he caused her drove Frederick to massive lusting. He sent his groin to her from every possible angle, thrilling to the feel of his organ in her diminutive bowel. His balls swung violently, knocking against her quaking cunt. He sawed and thrust and hunched in passionate frenzy. He heard her crying; he could not be gentle, so afire were his balls and so alive was his prick. And when he felt his cum approaching, he grew even wilder, lifting her knees from the grass with his total rooting. When it burst, he had a moment of frightful agony as his raw cock tried to escape its lacerated skin. The cum was short, weaker than he wanted. He settled over Mary's back, panting, half blacked out by strain and weariness. His prick softened quickly, and Mary crawled from under him, moaning in agony. On hands and knees, his shit-brown cock hanging straight down, its deflated head dripping watery cum, he rested. His lungs fought for breath, his belly heaved. He could neither see nor hear and he remained so, like a dog defeated by a fleeter rabbit. He seemed to Mary to be properly helpless.

Mary climbed slowly to her feet, her asshole vomiting, her hip paining with mortal agony. Standing, she could not straighten her back. She looked down at the naked man and saw him weaving. One slow step at a time, she went to where the buggy whip lay in the grass. She picked it up but not by the butt. Her hands stretched the meter long lash of rawhide; she made a wrap around each of her fists. Then she moved to stand at Master Tensington's side. Controlling her scream of agony, she straddled his back. With all the speed and strength she could muster, she looped the rawhide twice around his neck and clamped herself to his abruptly jerking body.

It took a long time for him to die. It took nearly as long for Mary to unclench her legs and arms and wriggle free of his limp body. She climbed to her feet and staggered toward the pony cart. But she passed it, her mind somehow incapable of thinking. She hobbled, a step and a drag because her hip was sprung again. After interminable ages, she came to the burned-out house.

Gasping, crying, she made her way into the tangle of ashes and charcoaled sticks.

She sat down on the ash-covered hearth, doubled over and hugged her legs and she cried then, once more a very little girl.

eleven

Marlene looked back once, in time to see the gables and chimney pots of Tensington fading in the dust from the carriage wheels. The joy she should have felt at this final good-bye was somehow missing. When she again straightened around, she met Malcomb Fageol's half smile and she tried to respond to the handsome man slouched across from her. Then the pop of a whip, the driver's, came like a pistol shot. She shuddered. Up on the driver's seat, Jan Macklin would be braced, his eyes narrowed to the wind, his huge hands controlling the reins, and thusly, her destiny for another three or four hours.

Her mind was saturated with panic. She could hardly believe that she sat now, elegantly garbed in maroon silk, with fine lace at throat and cuff, her hair coiled high and fitted to the broad-brimmed hat so delightfully stylish only a week or so ago. She tried not to think of the seemingly unending nightmare she had lived for two days, but the carriage wheels rolling over the less than perfect road set up a rhythmic jolting that enlivened every bruise and wound on her weary body. She looked down at her gloved fingers nervously intertwining. The whip popped again, accompanied by a "Ho-hah!" in a voice Marlene thought she would never live long enough to forget.

Across from her, Malcomb shifted his long legs and tipped his head back to rest on the seat back. Unwilling to look right or left at the green countryside, Marlene stared straight ahead. And after several minutes, she discovered she was staring at Malcomb's lethargic hips, and that the abandon of his legs drew the fine serge of his gray trousers in ugly tightness about his thighs. His cock lay like a country sausage along the inner seam and above that, his ball bulged in vulgar rounds. Marlene blinked. Again the whip popped. She quivered unreasonably.

It would always be so, she believed. Tensington was past and if she ever learned to be half calm about her horrid experiences there, the certainty that half of the population of England was masculine, and thusly equipped with the insidious flesh-pole and its inevitable source of venality, the wrinkled sack of sperm-makers, would remain as a threat to her sanity.

It jiggled slightly to the carriage sway, settling its shape in the cloth with firmer design. She could detect the small ridge of the languid foreskin, and the significant knot of the flaccid head. It would be warm, nested as it was against the probably hairy thigh. Toward the base where it joined his flat abdomen, the shaft would show fine tendrils of brown curly hair. She swallowed heavily. It was all only a guess. She could not remember even seeing a prick in repose; all those presented to her in the last two days had been hard and thrusting and throbbing with lust. Frederick's had been long and slim, with a broadly flared head that gleamed brightly with pumping blood. How long had it been? Marlene's hands formed together in double gripping and her belly crawled with memory. With the soft-layered hardness well back to her throat, there had yet been a hand of rigid shaft between her pursed lips and his hairy groin. The whip popped out over the team again. Not as long as Jan Macklin's nor as thick. Momentarily, she closed her eyes, the vision of his gigantic organ smothering her brain. It was made of iron rods planted in his belly, and the steel hardness thickened half way to the incredible bludgeon at the tip. The head was wide and thick, with the finely formed coronal ridge a fitting collar for the royal bluntness. Even distended, there was massive slack in the dead white skin, shaded by the traceries of pulsating veins. Marlene's eyes opened to dispel the vision. Another memory crushed to prominence: Tillie's voice, "—God made woman a weak and wanting thing with no strength to resist abominations she knows will give her pleasure!"

Marlene leaned forward and placed her gloved hand on the ridge in Malcomb's trousers. He jerked from a half doze, and she smiled, the feel of the sausage shape causing her blood to race.

"My dear!" he exclaimed in pleased surprise.

"Oh, Malcomb, Malcomb!" she panted and went to her knees between his finely booted feet. With great deliberation, she removed the two long hatpins and laid her flowered hat aside. Then she opened his jacket and unsnapped his galluses. After that, the fly of his trousers. She saw gleefully that the lethargic prick was no longer lazy. It was distending and rising, building a significant bulge in the restraining trouser leg. One by one, she removed her gloves, folding them precisely to lay them with her hat. Then she inserted her slim hand and he shifted so she could swing his cock around and up out of his clothes. It was a fine organ, thick and long enough. She frigged it lightly, staring at the way the head jerked when she dragged back the foreskin and thrilling to its instant urging.

The whip popped twice. "Ho-had!" came the groundskeeper's bark. Marlene lowered her head, lips pursed, tongue darting to the vertical eye of the abomination she could not resist. As she took the hot column into her mouth, Malcomb gasped and put his hands to her head. He leaned as she let the throbbing pole slide deep to the back of her mouth, tongue under in pulsating pressure. His hands slid down her face to her neck, feeling for a moment the convulsions of her throat, then moving on to slide into the neck of her dress and the up-bulge of her corseted tits.

Above the rumble of the carriage and the hiss of Malcomb's breath, she could hear Tillie's voice, patiently weary, trembling with excitement as she explained the pure ecstacies of detached sex. Marlene understood; the cock in her mouth, hot, responsive, delighted with her affection, was the other half of being a woman. The hands fondling her tits belonged to Malcomb Fageol, but the prick was hers, to bathe in saliva and urge its surrender as she chose. She chose. Her head bobbed faster, her lips closed fiercely and she could feel the response of Malcomb's hips, fucking up to her absorption with straining.

"Marlene, M-Marlene! I'm going to cum. Oh! Oh! Oh!"

She raised slightly, holding the swelling head in her lips. The jism came in needle sharp spurts, striking the back of her throat, then her updrawn tongue and as it spewed, she rolled the thick musk in her mouth and reluctantly swallowed it. The fire went straight down to her weeping quim and she had a soft, exquisitely deep orgasm that joined the throbbing in her mouth. With an under-thumbing, she stripped the relaxing tube from balls to tip and sucked in the final oozing glob. Then she lay the softening prick to her face and closed her eyes as she worked her slime filled mouth and swallowed in eager gluttony. She thought, poor Tillie, who loved this so and I have killed her forever. I cannot let her die in vain.

It was awkward and the coach jiggled. They laughed, but still they strove. Marlene lay on her hip, her shoulder resting on the seat back. Malcomb, in the same position, his revitalized cock a standing promise, gathered Marlene's dress and three petticoats high around her waist. Her bloomers, sagged about her shoe-tops, somewhat constricted her leg freedom, but as they squirmed together, his prick managed to nudge and separate the lips of her flaming cunt.

"No, I cannot get it in, Marlene," he panted. "The confounded carriage jiggles so and the seat is too fucking narrow!"

"Then I will turn and double! Oh, Malcomb, you must get that divine tool into my quim! I cannot stand it longer. Wait!"

She twisted out of his arm and turned, to fold over onto the seat, her bare rump raised and thrust back. He wriggled, finding the deep divide between the cheeks of her ass and thrusting on. The jolt of the coach was sometimes advantageous, sometimes frustrating, but when his prick was thoroughly imbedded in her gripping quim, the bounding of the carriage was like an extra blessing. Malcomb had never been randier in his life. He smashed his groin to the cheeks of her ass, gripping her hips to hold her to his thrust. He knew his trousers would be ruined by her cunt juices, and later, by his fuming jism but he did not care. His shirt was wet with sweat and his boots were scuffed. He fucked the beautiful bottom, wincing at the way it pinched his cock at every undulation. Some minutes past, he had ceased to wonder at the way in which Marlene de la Sage had come onto him, the same frenzied nymph she had been in the Fedren cottage. Crouching hard to her, he could hear her moaning and pleading, "Fuck me, fuck me, fuck me! Harder, deeper! Oh, split me in two! I must hurt, I have to bleed! Malcomb, fuck me harder!" And he tried, grunting and hunching and drooling saliva to the folds of her gathered dress. Once or twice, he was sure she had cum, but the fever-writhing and back-rearing did not slacken and he fought on to spew his jism in her gulping quim. And suddenly, he was jerked back from the edge of bursting orgasm.

The coach slowed. He heard the whine of brake shoes, then the voice of the driver coaxing the team to a halt. Fighting for sanity, Malcomb dragged his streaming prick from the still humping ass and tried to straighten up. "Marlene. The carriage has stopped! Marlene!" he whispered. He was still struggling to get his trousers up and buttoned when the thump of two big feet sounded on the ground. His cock was unwilling to fold away, his galluses were high and out of place.

"Malcomb, Malcomb, why have you stopped?" Marlene wailed.

"Oh, for the love of God!" he swore, but it was too late.

Jan Macklin, his dusty felt at a rakish angle was staring in through the coach window. His eyes were narrowed, hard, his face a granite mask. He looked at Malcomb's half limp cock, then at the broad bare ass so beautifully surrounded by petticoat frills and maroon silk. He snapped the coach door open and his huge fist came in to close around Malcomb's arm. Malcomb yelped at the steel grip, then he was jerked. He bumped the door casing as he flew, and when Jan Macklin hurled him, he skidded out on the half-grass, half-dirt field. He opened his mouth to protest and the whip popped at his groin. His scream was mortal as he saw half the head of his prick disappear, to be replaced by a thick fountain of blood. Crazed with pain and frenzied with terror, he turned over and tried to crawl away. The whip cut his buttock through the serge trousers. Malcomb went down at the third slashing; for a split moment, his mind was very clear, and very very certain that Jan Macklin meant to kill him with the whip, exactly as he had shredded Tillie Fedren.

He didn't have Tillie's courage, Jan decided. The fop lay quietly, only his fingers clutching into the dirt. The trail of blood from where he had begun his bleeding was short. Tillie had crawled clear across the cottage floor with her mouth split from ear to ear. He tore the fancy trousers from waist to crotch with a particular plucking stroke of the whip. Spindle bottom, he mused. Then he remembered another bottom. Turning, he saw that Marlene had regained some composure and had descended from the carriage. She lay back in horror against the open door, her bodice disarranged to expose one bulbous tit and her skirt and petticoats not yet down around her legs.

"Well now," he said. "I think we have some unfinished business, do we not, my pretty-assed friend?" He grinned as her head turned from side to side. "No. While your puny friend was warming your lovely bottom, I left the road to rest the horses and evade a passing highwayman. Now, you see, I have become a hero. I have saved the beautiful Marlene de la Sage from being raped by a madman!"

"Yes! Yes," she hissed. "He was raping me! He wrestled me down and tore my clothes open! He raped me! I am distraught!"

Jan chuckled, his eyes devouring her disheveled beauty. Her coiffure had broken and her thick auburn hair hung over one shoulder in perfect compliment to her quivering bare tit. The maroon silk glistened in the sunlight and her finely heeled, high button shoes made neat pedestals for her voluptuous form. He wanted her more than he had ever wanted any woman, but he

wanted her his way, screaming and groveling, her white
flesh streaked with his whip fury, her sex burned to a
white hot flame only his jism could douse. He rustled
the whip on the ground and her eyes followed it as if it
were an angry snake.

"Take off your clothes, woman," he said heavily.

"What!" she gasped. "You fiend!" Then she made a
hasty move to tuck her tit back into her bodice. Jan
sent the whip out and around her wrist, and his jerk
brought her spinning into his clutches. Her curses and
struggles were nothing. He tore her gown down the
back, then holding her arm up so she nearly dangled,
proceeded to rip it away, and then the petticoats. Her
bloomers, not quite in place, came away with another
mighty snatching. He spun her out, wearing only the
short corset to which her long hose were snapped. The
pink garment, flared and lace-edged, ended at the swell
of her naked hips. Its upper form bulged her tits up in
high rolls. Half crouched in terror, her hairy crotch
gleamed with suspicious wetness. He took a step and
claimed her left ankle and his jerk upended her. She fell
to her back, breathless, her legs apart, her cunt gaping
prettily in the sun. Jan methodically opened his breeches
and took out his prick. It was half-hard and swelling; he
let it arch out, untouched, a mighty threat becoming
mightier. Then her turned and whip-bit a fleck of flesh
from the fop's bare bottom. Marlene screamed, as if
it had been her ass he had bloodied. The man only
groaned and tried to crawl a little. His bleeding cock,
dragging back between his thighs, made a line of red
mud. Jan changed the technique of his whip. The fop
was alive and that was the way Jan wanted him, sensitive, responsive and able to suffer. He lay the whip

right and left over the writing body, saving the bite and snap for a later ecstacy.

The fever came to Jan as it had the day before when he had reduced Tillie to a shuddering, bleeding huddle. His cock, now ramrod stiff, swayed and bobbed as he strained to every whip stroke. He could hear Marlene screaming, and to his right, the shuffling and snorting of the team. The sun was hot; he stole a moment to remove his jacket and catch new breath in his raw lungs. Then he lashed with renewed fury, delighting in every twinge and jerk the fop made after each blow. Then a different shiriek, a nearly animal sound, made him turn toward Marlene.

She stood in a spraddle-legged stance, her hips pushed forward so her cunt was raised. He could see the deep under-rounds of her ass, close pressed in straining. Her corset was lying on the grass, discarded with the same frenzied fingers that now rolled and pulled at her massive tits.

"Fuck me!" she screamed. "Fuck me with the whip, the whip! Oh God, I cannot stand it! Fuck me, like you did poor Tillie!"

Jan's eyes narrowed and he took a long step toward her. His whip whistled, and he cut a long, scarlet line across her out-thrust belly, just above the bush of pubic hair.

"Oh God! Yes, yes, yes!" she screeched, throwing her arms out so that her tits lay thick and jouncing on her back-tilted chest. "Like Tillie, like Tillie! Fuck me to death with the whip!"

He laid a cross on her belly; she screamed with endless breath but her stance did not change nor waver, like a steer, he thought, stunned by a sledge blow at the

ase of the skull. Laughter came from his throat in a
'uttering groan, his lips rolled high and low and saliva
rooled from his open mouth. When her scream seemed
to soften, he drew more red lines on her white flesh,
from thoat to knees. Then he began to step sideways,
like a fencer, the whip moving its slash around her body
until the twin moons of her writhing ass were the delectable targets. He bit each one delicately. Marlene
straightened, her arms going high, fingers wiggling like
tortured worms. Now she slowly bended forward until
her ass spread wide. Then she reached back and curled
her fingers deep into the pillowy flesh of her nates and
pulled them apart until the valley seemed ready to split.
Stunned, Jan stared at the dark rosebud of her bum
hold, and below it, the haired rolls of cunt, wet and
quaking.

He stepped forward, unbelting as he moved. He was
close to the spread nates before his breeches sagged.
His prick was up in a rigid angle, the veins throbbing as
they pumped furiously to burst the thick foreskin. Still
holding his whip firmly, he kinked his knees and drove
his cock into the glistening cunt with a mighty lunge.
Marlene screeched at the monstrous attack. She let go
of her ass and caught herself as she tumbled forward,
but Jan's weight made her elbows fold and she went to
her knees, back down-arched to rear her ass to his
crushing weight. Clutching her hips, he fucked furiously
for only a moment before his cum exploded and spewed.
He churned madly, feeling the sticky slime squirt back
onto his balls as her quim gripped and milked around
his gigantic cock.

"No, no, the whip, Jan!" she cried. "Fuck me with
the whip!"

Still gripping the butt, he caught two loops with curling fingers and his arm raised and fell as he thrashed her back with the shorter fronds. She moaned and humped, still impaled on his member, and he felt no slackening in its rigidity. Marlene spread her elbows and went to the dirt on her shoulders. Jan saw how his prick coursed in her cunt, above that the winking, twitching bud of her bum hole. With renewed lust, he jerked his organ from her vagina and fed it to the rubbery pecker. It seemed tight, but it loosened with each flail of the whip, and when he could wait no longer, he grunted and lunged. His prick took the ringlet in until it seemed he had punched a new hole in her flesh. He fucked furiously, his arm rising and falling in rhythm to his stroking. Her back turned pink, then deeper scarlet and the frenzy of her head, rolling from side to side caused her hair to stir small wisps of dust.

Malcomb had ceased to feel. Numbness spread from his destroyed prick through his belly and to each wound Jan Macklin had left. He could crawl and he did, his eyes only flicking the obscene drama of hammering belly to spraddle ass. He crawled slowly, aiming for open door of the carriage, a blurry image in the shimmering sun. But if he had ceased to feel, his mind had not surrendered to despair. Even if he lived, he would never fuck again, and he was sure he could never stand erect, so brutally had his back been slashed. At the carriage step, his strength gave away. He prayed and wept and finally managed to hoist his tortured body up. He stretched out a bloody hand, hunched a bit farther, then sighed as his fingers closed around the handle of his totebag. He dragged it to him and blubbers of hope escaped his lips. The catch was stubborn, but now he had acquired the patience of the doomed. Presently, the brass mouth opened and he stilled, staring into the mass of toilet jars, mixed with kerchiefs and pomades. Then he fumbled into the contents and found the gun. He had never fired it, except in testing. It had cost twelve pounds and was the latest five shot revolver made by the up and coming firm of Smith and Wesson. Malcomb held the weapon in his trembling hand. His thumb would not bring back the hammer; he knew he had not the strength to fire the weapon double-action. He used his left hand to drag the hammer back.

Turning then, he leaned on the carriage casing. His trousers were now down around his ankles. His blood was smeared from navel to knee and it still pumped from the demolished head of his penis. He looked out to where the groundskeeper knelt, his thundering cock now coursing brutally in Marlene's rectum, his arm rising and falling. The slap of the bunched whip was loud. Malcomb raised the pistol and tried to steady it on the broad back. It wouldn't do, he knew. The back seemed to shift, his hand would not steady. And a bullet where it was not fatal would only turn the monster into a raving killer. He writhed erect and tried to take a step. His trousers hobbled him effectively but Malcomb knew he did not have the strength, nor the time to bend and removed them, or even drag them up. Shuffling, his eyes glued to the humping body, he moved closer and closer.

And finally, he was close enough to hear the slosh-slosh of the huge cock in Marlene de la Sage's rectum. He could hear her moans, Jan Macklin's grunts. He raised the pistol and was pleased that his hand was steadier and the back less shifty. His forefinger wrapped around the trigger would not move. He strained, then he prayed, and as his total strength dissolved, he breathed, "Please God!" and with the thunder of the gun, a neat hole appeared in the base of Jan Macklin's skull.

Malcomb tumbled to the ground. His blood-starved body twitched once or twice but he was dead before he had time to thank his Maker.

twelve

Marlene crawled slowly from under the huge weight on her back. She felt the deflated thing slip from her asshole but it didn't seem to matter. Half free, she twisted, her mouth open to ask him why he had so abruptly ceased his loving her. His shaggy head lay on her leg, the blood from somewhere trickled around her neck and made a bright red rivulet among the many less vivid lines. She frowned and climbed to her feet, jism dripping from her cunt, her own excrement gushing from her ruptured rectum to form malodorous streams down her quavering legs. She saw the other man and was surprised.

She looked around and her eyes hesitated on nothing. Somewhere. It had to be close by. Then she saw it coiled half under the still man with blood coming from his head. She knelt and worked it from the lifeless fingers. It was heavy and thick in her hand. She let it uncoil, then she raised the butt and pressed it to her lips. Her tongue caressed the worn plaiting, licked at the sweat moist and the fine dust.

At last it was hers. She rubbed it to her cheeks, to her throat, and then to her red-laced tits and belly. It seemed alive. It breathed on her flesh with delightful fire. At last, it was hers.

The sun seemed very hot on her head. Perspiration ran down from her tousled hair and, where it touched a sweetly raw stripe, caused a marvelous stinging. She looked around and not too far away, a thicket appeared, and behind and over it, a huge green tree. She thought it would be cooler there. Her whip would like it better, too. She stumbled forward, then discovered the trailing lash was accumulating dirt on its blood-stained extremity.

Marlene stopped and gathered the long trailing leather. Then she held the loose coils in her left hand and with a giggle of glee, stuffed the thick butt into her vagina, wriggled pleasurably and wandered off into the thicket.

My Secret Life—Anonymous
Anonymous

Over two million copies sold!

Perhaps the most infamous of all underground Victorian erotica, *M* *Secret Life* is the sexual memoir of a well-to-do gentleman, who began at an early age to keep a diary of his erotic behavior. He con tinues this record for over forty years, creating in the process unique social and psychological document. Its complete and detailed description of the hidden side of British and European life in the nine teenth century furnishes materials for the understanding of the Victorian Age that cannot be duplicated in from any other source.

———

The Altar of Venus
Anonymous

Our author, a gentleman of wealth and privilege, is introduced to desire's delights at a tender age, and then and there commits himsel to a life-long sensual expedition. As he enters manhood, he pro gresses from schoolgirls' charms to older women's enticements, espe cially those of acquaintances' mothers and wives. Later, he move beyond common London brothels to sophisticated entertainment available only in Paris. Truly, he has become a lord among libertines

———

Caning Able
Stan Kent

Caning Able is a modern-day version of the melodramatic tales of Victorian erotica. Full of dastardly villains, regimented discipline corporal punishment and forbidden sexual liaisons, the novel fea tures the brilliant and beautiful Jasmine, a seemingly helpless heroine who reigns triumphant despite dire peril. By mixing libidinous prose with a changing business world, *Caning Able* gives treasured plots a welcome twist: women who are definitely not the weaker sex.

The Blue Moon Erotic Reader IV

A testimonial to the publication of quality erotica, *The Blue Moon Erotic Reader IV* presents more than twenty romantic and exciting excerpts from selections spanning a variety of periods and themes. This is a historical compilation that combines generous extracts from the finest forbidden books with the most extravagant samplings that the modern erotica imagination has created. The result is a collection that is provocative, entertaining, and perhaps even enlightening. It encompasses memorable scenes of youthful initiations into the mysteries of sex, notorious confessions, and scandalous adventures of the powerful, wealthy, and notable. From the classic erotica of *Wanton Women*, and *The Intimate Memoirs of an Edwardian Dandy* to modern tales like Michael Hemmingson's *The Rooms*, good taste, passion, and an exalted desire are abound, making for a union of sex and sensibility that is available only once in a Blue Moon.

With selections by Don Winslow, Ray Gordon, M. S. Valentine, P. N. Dedeaux, Rupert Mountjoy, Eve Howard, Lisabet Sarai, Michael Hemmingson, and many others.

The Best of the Erotic Reader

"The Erotic Reader series offers an unequaled selection of the hottest scenes drawn from the finest erotic writing."—*Elle*

This historical compilation contains generous extracts from the world's finest forbidden books including excerpts from *Memories of a Young Don Juan*, *My Secret Life*, *Autobiography of a Flea*, *The Romance of Lust*, *The Three Chums*, and many others. They are gathered together here to entertain, and perhaps even enlighten. From secret texts to the scandalous adventures of famous people, from youthful initiations into the mysteries of sex to the most notorious of all confessions, *Best of the Erotic Reader* is a stirring complement to the senses. Containing the most evocative pieces covering several eras of erotic fiction, *Best of the Erotic Reader* collects the most scintillating tales from the seven volumes of *The Erotic Reader*. This comprehensive volume is sure to include delights for any taste and guaranteed to titillate, amuse, and arouse the interests of even the most veteran erotica reader.

Confessions D'Amour
Anne-Marie Villefranche

Confessions D'Amour is the culmination of Villefranche's comically indecent stories about her friends in 1920s' Paris.

Anne-Marie Villefranche invites you to enter an intoxicating world where men and women arrange their love affairs with skill and style. This is a world where illicit encounters are as smooth as a silk stocking, and where sexual secrets are kept in confidence only until a betrayal can be turned to advantage. Here we follow the adventures of Gabrielle de Michoux, the beautiful young widow who contrives to be maintained in luxury by a succession of well-to-do men, Marcel Chalon, ready for any adventure so long as he can go home to Mama afterwards, Armand Budin, who plunges into a passionate love affair with his cousin's estranged wife, Madelein Beauvais, and Yvonne Hiver who is married with two children while still embracing other, younger lovers.

"An erotic tribute to the Paris of yesteryear that will delight modern readers."—*The Observer*

A Maid For All Seasons I, II – Devlin O'Neill

Two Delightful Tales of Romance and Discipline

Lisa is used to her father's old-fashioned discipline, but is it fair that her new employer acts the same way? Mr. Swayne is very handsome, very British and very particular about his new maid's work habits. But isn't nineteen a bit old to be corrected that way? Still, it's quite a different sensation for Lisa when Mr. Swayne shows his displeasure with her behavior. But Mr. Swayne isn't the only man who likes to turn Lisa over his knee. When she goes to college she finds a new mentor, whose expectations of her are even higher than Mr. Swayne's, and who employs very old-fashioned methods to correct Lisa's bad behavior. Whether in a woodshed in Georgia, or a private club in Chicago, there is always someone there willing and eager to take Lisa in hand and show her the error of her ways.

ORDER FORM
Attach a separate sheet for additional titles.

Title	Quantity	Price
_____	_____	_____
_____	_____	_____
_____	_____	_____
_____	_____	_____

Shipping and Handling (see charges below) _____

Sales tax (in CA and NY) _____

Total _____

Name _____

Address _____

City _____ State _____ Zip _____

Daytime telephone number _____

❑ Check   ❑ Money Order   (US dollars only. No COD orders accepted.)

Credit Card # _____ Exp. Date _____

❑ MC   ❑ VISA   ❑ AMEX

Signature _____

(if paying with a credit card you must sign this form.)

Shipping and Handling charges:*

Domestic: $4 for 1st book, $.75 each additional book. International: $5 for 1st book, $1 each additional book.
*rates in effect at time of publication. Subject to Change.

Mail order to Publishers Group West, Attention: Order Dept., 1700 Fourth St., Berkeley, CA 94710
or fax to (510) 528-3444.

PLEASE ALLOW 4-6 WEEKS FOR DELIVERY. ALL ORDERS SHIP VIA 4TH CLASS MAIL.

**Look for Blue Moon Books at your favorite local bookseller
or from your favorite online bookseller.**